Success!

Swaying her minisk
seductive movement that captured the
attention of every male in the room,
La Rubia glided through customs to a
waiting taxi.

*If only the general would succumb to her
charms as easily as the customs officer!*
"The Hotel de la Revolución, *por favor*," she
told the driver.

"La Rubia's wish is my command."

She knew that deep voice instantly. Once,
in another time, Mitch Cantrell's voice had
possessed the power to thrill her to the
core. *It still did.*

Mitch's grin, reflected in the rearview
mirror, was dazzling. "The Tory Martin I
knew wore baggy fatigues," Mitch
continued as he looked her over, "although
I *do* like that sexy skirt."

Tory remembered. They'd been two
reporters thrown together in the middle of
a civil war. It had been inevitable that
they'd make love. What she hadn't counted
on was falling in love.

*Or on Mitch appearing on the scene now,
ready to ruin her plans!*

Dear Reader,

Here it is, the much-in-demand spin-off of Temptation #333, *Tangled Hearts*. When JoAnn Ross sent Mitch Cantrell off into the turmoil of Central America alone, she realized his story wasn't finished. She had a wonderful hero—strong willed, but wounded by love—who needed an equally strong woman who could challenge and love him. Who could be more perfect than Tory Martin, a beautiful woman risking her own life for her sister? For extra measure, JoAnn threw in a steamy climate, a corrupt general and a dangerous intrigue and let the fireworks ignite!

We'd love to hear from you about *Tangled Hearts* and *Tangled Lives*. Please take the time to write to us.

The Editors
Harlequin Temptation
225 Duncan Mill Road
Don Mills, Ontario, Canada
M3B 3K9

Tangled Lives

JoAnn Ross

Harlequin Books

TORONTO • NEW YORK • LONDON
AMSTERDAM • PARIS • SYDNEY • HAMBURG
STOCKHOLM • ATHENS • TOKYO • MILAN

Published May 1991

ISBN 0-373-25445-8

TANGLED LIVES

Printed in U.S.A.

1

HER REPUTATION had preceded her.

For weeks the men of the Central American country of La Paz gathered in smoke-filled cantinas and talked of little else. Her long golden hair glowed like filament, her voice, half honey, half smoke, was guaranteed to kindle the inner fires of any man with blood still stirring in his veins. Indeed, even the archbishop, a much-admired cleric in his late seventies, was rumored to have said that La Rubia—the blonde—was the first woman to have ever made him reconsider his lifelong vow of celibacy.

And her body.... *¡Dios mío!* The men would breathe a collective sigh, their appreciative gazes drifting to the posters announcing her upcoming singing engagement at the Hotel de la Revolución tacked on the cantina wall. Those lush curves were not those of a mere mortal woman; they belonged to a goddess. But her face, with its fiery emerald eyes surrounded by thick black lashes, was that of a witch.

Witch? Or goddess?

Bruja? Or *diosa?*

Which was La Rubia?

Many men in La Paz would have given their right arm to discover the truth for themselves. But everyone knew that only one would claim her. General José Enrique Ramirez. The man who ruled the country with an iron fist. Those foolish enough to cross Ramirez had a bad way of turning up dead. Or of becoming one of the *Desaparecidos*—the disappeared ones.

So, enticing though La Rubia was, no man in the country was prepared to challenge his leader for her favors. Instead they sat around scarred wooden tables, smoking cigars, drinking tequila, trading rumors about her many lovers and making drunken boasts about their own bedroom skills. Then much, much later they returned home to their wives and fantasized that they were making love to La Rubia.

Mitchell Cantrell, crack television foreign correspondent and reluctant American hero, had been in Central America twelve months, in La Paz for six weeks, when posters of La Rubia began appearing on fences, walls and buses all over the capital city of Playa de Palma.

She was clad in a floor-length black velvet dress; the plunging neckline revealed a dazzling amount of pearly flesh. Contrasting with the lush black velvet, her golden blond hair cascaded to her waist. Her ruby lips were glossed and parted invitingly in a provocative pout.

But it was her eyes that captured the viewer's attention. They glowed like emerald fire. Mitch had seen those same vivid eyes spark with intelligence. Over a stormy three-month period he'd seen them blaze with temper and soften with passion. But in all that time he'd never once witnessed the intensity the photographer had captured. The pose was blatantly sexy, but it was not seduction Mitch saw in those remarkable, but unfamiliar green eyes.

It was murder.

He tossed back his tequila and gestured for the bartender to pour him another. "What the hell is she up to now?" he wondered out loud. The bartender, accustomed to the Yankee newsman's habit of talking to himself, didn't answer.

THE CUSTOMS OFFICER had the same grim, granite face perfected by his contemporaries all over the world. If she couldn't make it past him, her entire scheme would fall apart before it got off the ground.

She watched him grill an elderly woman. The retired primary school principal had been her seatmate on the flight to Playa de Palma, during which time the woman had spoken proudly of her work for the Peace Corps. She'd come to La Paz filled with optimistic plans to help the impoverished children of the barrio, but from the way the customs official was treating her, she could have been a participant in a plot to overthrow the government.

La Rubia's pulse was racing; despite a temperature in the nineties, with a humidity just as high, her hands were ice-cold. Heart pounding, she checked her appearance in her compact mirror, relieved when her reflection failed to reveal her anxiety.

Apparently unsatisfied with the older woman's answers, the man called for a soldier, who practically dragged the former principal away down a long hallway. There had once been a time when she would have immediately leaped to her travel companion's defense, even if it had meant starting World War III. But she was playing for higher stakes this time; she couldn't risk tipping her hand.

The long line slowly snaked its way across the dreary dark basement of the airport until it was her turn to face the inquisition. Taking a deep breath, she tossed her gilt mane over her shoulder, tugged her white silk blouse a little lower and flashed the uniformed man her most dazzling smile.

He recognized her immediately. His eyes widened and a dark red flush rose from the collar of his khaki uniform. "La Rubia."

"My real name is Pandora Cavanaugh," she corrected in the soft, breathy voice invented by Marilyn Monroe—an imitation La Rubia had perfected by renting a videotape of *Gentlemen Prefer Blondes* and watching it over and over again. She leaned toward the man, allowing her scent to envelop him in a heady, fragrant cloud of jasmine and roses. "But if you'd prefer, *señor*, you may call me by my professional name of La Rubia."

The blush moved over his dark features like a fever. His eyes didn't move from hers as he accepted her passport.

So far, so good. La Rubia waited impatiently for him to return her papers, but he seemed too mesmerized to move. Or, for that matter, to speak. "Is that all?" she asked finally.

He shook his head as if to clear it. "I apologize for having kept you waiting," he said formally. He quickly stamped the back of her visa. When he returned the passport, his fingers brushed against hers. "Welcome to La Paz, La Rubia. If there is anything I can do to make your visit more pleasant, please do not hesitate to ask. My name is Juan. Juan Martinez."

His dark eyes, gleaming with blatant hope, reminded her of a cocker spaniel. "Thank you, Juan," she breathed. "There is just one little thing. . . ."

"Anything," he answered promptly.

"If you could tell me where I could arrange for transportation to my hotel, I would so appreciate it. My agent assured me that he would have a limousine waiting, but . . ." Her bare shoulders lifted and dropped in a faint, feminine shrug.

From his disappointed expression, it was obvious that the customs officer had been hoping for a more personal request. "There is a taxi stand just outside the door," he said flatly.

"Thank you." Another smile. By the time she finally got out of this horrid place, her lips would be frozen in place. She slipped a folded bill into his hand. "You've been most helpful." Then, caught up in her role, she tacked on, "I have always been dependent on the kindness of strangers."

With that she walked away, followed by a uniformed porter pushing a cart loaded with her luggage. Her hips—clad in a black leather miniskirt—swayed in a smooth, seductive movement that captured the attention of every male in the room.

Success! Walking into the blazing sunshine, she had to restrain herself from shouting out her relief. She'd made it past the first hurdle. The next step was to pull off tonight's performance in front of the general. General José Enrique Ramirez was the key. If she couldn't snare him, her entire trip would turn out to be an exercise in futility.

"No," she muttered to herself as she handed the porter a folded bill. "It's going to work. It has to work."

Engrossed in her plans, she slipped into the back seat of the nearest taxi.

"The Hotel de la Revolución, *por favor*," she told the driver absently while debating which dress to wear for her opening number. The black velvet contrasted nicely with her complexion and her new blond wig, but the red-beaded gown was decidedly sexier. And the general was reputed to like his women flashy. The red. She didn't have time for subtlety.

"La Rubia's wish is my command," the driver answered, pulling away from the curb.

It had been eight long years. But Tory Martin could never forget that deep voice. There was none like it anywhere in the world. Once, in another time, Mitchell Cantrell's voice had possessed the power to thrill her to the core. Today it sounded like trouble. With a capital *T*.

Tory groaned. "I don't believe this."

Mitch's grin, reflected in the rearview mirror, was every bit as dazzling as the ones she'd bestowed upon the customs officer. "Small world, isn't it?" he said cheerfully.

"It seems to be." The cab was not air-conditioned; Tory felt as if she were in a sauna. And the oppressive weight of the wig covering her own brunette hair didn't help. Fanning herself with her passport, she lifted the hair off the back of her neck.

"It'll take you a while to get used to this heat again," he said. "And you're not exactly dressed for the tropics. Although I do like that skirt."

"I'm so pleased that you approve."

Mitch ignored her sarcasm. "It's a definite improvement over those baggy fatigues you were wearing the last time I saw you."

He swerved abruptly to avoid hitting an army jeep that had suddenly pulled out in front of him. The streets were filled with military vehicles, Tory noticed. Which wasn't all that surprising, considering that La Paz was a military dictatorship. General Ramirez had been promising elections since he'd taken over the country eight years ago in a short-lived, but bloody revolution. Unsurprisingly he'd continued to stall while grasping power for himself, until any dreams of democracy the people of La Paz might have entertained had long since faded away.

"We were in the middle of a war zone," Tory reminded him. "I couldn't exactly wear a ball gown. Besides, you weren't decked out in a top hat and tails, Mitchell Cantrell. You were wearing the same fatigues I was."

"True. But they looked a lot better on you."

His voice deepened momentarily, making Tory wonder exactly how much he remembered about those months they'd spent together. They'd been two foreign reporters, far away from home, thrown together by fate into the middle of a civil war. Later, with the twenty-twenty vision of hindsight, Tory had come to the conclusion that since danger was a proven aphrodisiac, it had been inevitable that they'd make love. What she hadn't counted on was falling in love.

They passed the next few blocks in silence. A pungent, smoky-dark cloud hovered over the buildings, evidence that the farmers outside the city were still engaged in slash-and-burn agriculture. As she heard the battered green bus ahead of them sound its horn and saw it pull onto the sidewalk to pass a stalled car, Tory recalled how the rush-hour traffic in Playa de Palma had always reminded her of a bullfight, every car a dangerous charging beast, every pedestrian an unwilling torero.

"I'll tell you what," Mitch suggested suddenly, as if the idea had just occurred to him. "When we get to the hotel I'll buy you a tall cold drink and you can explain why Victoria Martin, crack AP foreign correspondent, has turned in her press card for a cabaret act." His grin widened, but Tory noticed that it didn't quite reach his eyes.

His blond hair might have silvered during their years apart, but his eyes were as vividly blue as she remembered. They also sparkled with the special glow that told her he was on the scent of a big story. She'd witnessed it innumerable times in the past. Only then she hadn't been his intended target.

"It's a long story," she murmured, slumping back onto the sticky, cracked vinyl seat.

"That's okay," Mitch assured her. "I'm not going anywhere."

As the taxi pulled to a stop in front of the hotel, Tory couldn't decide whether to take his words as a promise or a threat.

A plush red carpet had been laid from the curb into the lobby. A liveried doorman, his scarlet uniform adorned with gold braid and tasseled epaulets bowed low and opened the passenger door with all the flourish of a coachman at the Court of Saint James.

As Mitch followed Tory into the lobby—decorated in a haute-Caribbean resort style boasting shiploads of rattan and acres of pink marble—he couldn't believe the flurry of activity created by La Rubia's arrival. Practically the entire staff, from the manager down to the lowliest kitchen help, was on hand to greet the hotel's celebrity guest.

Also in attendance were the American ambassador to La Paz, the mayor of Playa de Palma, who gave her an oversize gilded key to the city, and the publisher of the country's largest and most influential newspaper, *La Libertad*, who kissed her hand in the continental fashion. Speeches were made; bouquets of sweet-smelling American Beauty roses were piled into her arms.

Behaving as if such accolades were an everyday occurrence, Tory responded in perfect Spanish. After declaring La Paz to be a most delightful and beautiful country, which unsurprisingly earned the enthusiastic applause of her audience, she thanked everyone for such a warm welcome. Then in a breathless voice that practically reeked of sex, she invited them all to attend the evening's performance.

Mitch, who had once heard Tory curse like a sailor when informed by armed guards that she couldn't go past their barricades into the war zone, couldn't help but be impressed by her performance. She might not be the Queen of Sheba or Princess Di, but La Rubia was damn sure the closest thing to royalty the citizens of La Paz were ever going to see.

Her little speech concluded, she turned to Mitch. "I suppose you may as well bring my luggage up to my room."

The Tory Martin he'd once known would have died before she'd allow a fellow correspondent to carry so much as a penknife for her. Mitch shook his head, wondering what had happened to the woman's any-thing-you-can-do, I-can-do-better attitude.

He knew that he could be accused of being a male chauvinist from time to time. Try as he might to be-come a modern, sensitive, understanding man, deep down inside he couldn't quite shake the belief that women were the softer, gentler sex. That being the case, why was it wrong to want to protect them from some of the more unattractive aspects of a male-dominated society?

Eight years ago, the majority of foreign correspon-dents had been male. Many of them were divorced due to the rigors of the job, others had never married. They worked hard, drank hard and took risks that only ob-sessed men would consider reasonable. And they damn well didn't believe that women reporters belonged in the field.

The ladies' place was at home, covering school-board elections and charity teas, one particularly vocal re-porter had insisted over drinks in the bar of the Playa de Palma Hilton. The other members of this closed fraternity had lifted their glasses, puffed on their cigars and agreed. Two days later, Tory Martin had arrived in La Paz.

After watching her work, Mitch had grudgingly ad-mitted that this particular woman at least, while re-markably green, seemed able to pull her weight. That being the case, he'd decided that perhaps women re-porters did have as much right to a story as he did. But just because he welcomed their competition didn't mean that he was willing to play nursemaid when the going got rough.

The only time he'd toted anything for a female reporter had been when Tory was injured diving for cover when a government helicopter suddenly appeared overhead, guns blazing. After the smoke had cleared and the photographers had gotten their shots of the dead and wounded, Mitch had hefted her over his shoulder and carried her out of the jungle.

Not that she'd asked for help. In fact she'd insisted that she was perfectly capable of walking back to Playa de Palma. Since the capital city was more than ten miles away, Mitch had been forced to muster his most persuasive tactics to win the argument. It also hadn't hurt when she'd fainted dead away after marching twenty-five yards on a broken ankle.

"Whatever you say, *señorita*," he said now. Hefting the garment bag over his shoulder, he picked up the remaining three pieces of flowered luggage and her cosmetic case and followed in the wake of her not inconsiderable entourage.

While the glass elevator made its ascent to the twenty-fifth floor of the new high-rise hotel, Tory continued to smile her Miss America smile, nod prettily and chatter on about how happy she was to be in such a marvelous country with such warm, wonderful people. All the time she was longing to get rid of all of them—especially Mitchell Cantrell. Unfortunately she knew Mitch well enough to realize that she was stuck with him for the duration. Unless she came up with a story he'd buy.

Fat chance. When she finally risked a glance at him, their eyes met and held and Tory knew that pulling the wool over this man's eyes would be difficult. Worse than difficult. It would be damn near impossible. But wasn't that what she was here to do? she asked herself. Accomplish the impossible?

The elevator doors opened. All the men backed up, allowing La Rubia to be the first to exit. On her heels were the ambassador, the mayor, the publisher and the hotel manager, followed by a host of lesser official dignitaries. Bringing up the rear was Mitch, loaded down with luggage and seemingly forgotten.

There was another little ceremony in the suite, where Tory was presented with still more flowers, a cellophane-wrapped basket of fruit and nuts and a chilled bottle of French champagne. More speeches were made; more photographs taken.

By the time everyone had left—including Mitch, she realized with surprise and relief—Tory was exhausted. Kicking off her high heels, she sank onto the sofa, put her feet up on the marble coffee table, leaned her head against the back of the sofa and closed her eyes.

During Tory's illustrious career she had scaled the mountains with the rebels in Afghanistan, slogged through the jungles in Panama, spent several days camped out with the student protesters in China's Tiananmen Square, ending that assignment dodging bullets and tanks when the government decided to crack down on the democracy movement. But never had she been as tired as she was now. Playing this alien sexpot role was obviously going to prove more stressful, more exhausting than she'd imagined. Not that she had any choice.

"Nice acting," that deep, all too familiar voice said. "If I hadn't known better, I would have thought you were actually enjoying that dog and pony show."

Tory kept her eyes closed for a long, silent moment, garnering strength. "I thought you'd left with the others." She didn't bother to hide her disappointment.

"Sorry. I thought I'd keep myself occupied until your band of merry men departed."

"Keep yourself occupied?" Anxiety skimmed up Tory's spine. "Doing what?"

"I was unpacking for you. Hey, you want the wrinkles to hang out of your clothes before tonight's performance, don't you?" he said quickly at her disapproving glare.

Tory knew he'd been searching her luggage. "I can unpack for myself."

He shrugged. "I do have just one little question."

"Only one? Now that's a switch."

"You're right. I've got a lot of questions. But the most compelling one right now is how many French nuns you suppose went blind making the lace on all that fancy underwear?"

"You were going through my underwear?"

"I was putting it away," he corrected. "And you know, if you'd worn that stuff back during our war days, I probably would have broken down and married you."

He was, Tory realized with surprise, the same old Mitch. Which was remarkable, considering all he'd been through.

"Gee, thanks," she said dryly. "But your memory's playing tricks on you, Cantrell. It was me who wouldn't marry you."

"Really?" Mitch frowned. "I could have sworn it was the other way around."

"Actually," Tory admitted, "neither of us was ready to get married in those days." But Mitch had married, Tory remembered. Two years after they'd separated. She'd been on assignment in East Germany at the time and had been surprised how much the news of his marriage had hurt.

A year later, on his first wedding anniversary, Mitch had been kidnapped by the Islamic jihad off the streets of Beirut. His bride, who had soon become an outspoken activist for the hostages, had reportedly witnessed the attack.

Two years after that, his holy-war captors had released a statement announcing the television newsman's execution for high crimes against Islam. Accompanying the statement was a photograph of a body, riddled with machine-gun holes. Although the photograph had been too blurry for positive identification, there was enough confirming evidence for the State Department to declare Mitchell Cantrell dead, despite the fact that his body was never recovered. The day the photo appeared on the front page of the *International Herald Tribune*, Tory had gotten drunk for the first—and last—time in her life.

Then a little over a year ago, he'd shown up at the American embassy in Beirut. Very much alive. Tory had been in Panama at the time. When she'd heard of Mitch's miraculous return from the dead, she'd immediately canceled her dinner date with an American army general and spent the night celebrating Mitch's release. Alone.

Looking at him now and remembering the bittersweet joy she'd felt that night, Tory's heart and eyes softened. "I really am glad those bastards didn't kill you," she said.

His answering smile was vintage Mitch. But there was a lingering depth of pain in his eyes that she'd never seen before. "Thanks. I'm glad they didn't kill me, too."

"I was going to call you," she admitted quietly. "But I didn't know what you'd told your wife about me—us—and I was afraid I'd put a damper on your home-coming."

Mitch laughed, but the sound held little humor. "Actually, I doubt if you could have made things any worse."

After Panama, Tory had been posted to the Soviet state of Lithuania, far away from easy access to American gossip. Now, as she observed the lines bracketing Mitch's mouth, she realized that she wasn't the only one with problems.

She was dying to ask if he was still married. But with the honesty that had always served her well, she admitted that a fiery twelve-week affair eight years ago didn't give her any rights where this man was concerned.

Besides, Tory reminded herself, she wasn't interested in Mitch Cantrell's personal life. She'd come here to do a job. Not to get embroiled in yet another ill-fated romance.

"I'm sorry," she said simply.

Mitch's only response was a shrug. He went over to the basket of fruit, unwrapped it, extracted a bright Red Delicious apple and wiped it on his jeans. Then he took a bite. "Mushy," he decided after he finished chewing. "Want to try an avocado?"

"I'm really not hungry," she declined with a shake of her head. "I think what I'd really like is a long soak in the tub and then a short nap before my performance."

Mitch tossed the unfinished apple into the wastebasket. "I'll start the water." He was halfway to the bathroom when his words sank in.

"I'd really like some time alone," she said pointedly.

With his hands in the pockets of his jeans, his stance was relaxed as he leaned against the doorjamb. "I'm afraid I can't allow that, Tory. Not until you tell me what this little charade is all about."

His voice was laced with a patience she'd never heard from him before. The Mitch Cantrell of her memory believed in a damn-the-torpedos-full-steam-ahead philosophy. Patience had certainly never been his strong suit.

But as Tory looked deep into his eyes, searching for a clue to this man who was at the same time familiar and strange, she realized that Mitch was prepared to wait all night, if that was what it took.

"All right," she said with a long-suffering sigh. "But if you're going to hang around, you may as well make yourself useful and order some coffee from room service."

Mitch studied her thoughtfully, thinking that beneath all that unfamiliar makeup she looked pale. A nap would probably do her good, he decided, opting not to push. For now. "You do know that decaf is considered heresy in this part of the world."

"Of course I do," she snapped back. "I have a very good memory. Besides, eight years isn't exactly an eternity."

"No. Sometimes it just seems like one." He gave her a long, unfathomable look. What was he thinking? she wondered as his silence and her frustration built.

What Tory had no way of knowing was that Mitch was thinking about all that lacy lingerie he'd put away earlier and wondering what she had on under that outrageously seductive blouse and skirt. That thought led to a memory of how she'd once felt in his arms. No matter what silky confection she might be wearing, he knew her skin would be softer.

"The point I was trying to make," he said finally, dragging his mind back to the subject at hand, "was that if you really want that nap, coffee might not be the best thing."

"On second thought I think I'll skip the nap," she told him, knowing she'd never be able to fall asleep, anyway. Not until after tonight's performance. Although it took an effort, she managed to flash him a smile that was almost a twin to the one she'd earlier bestowed upon the customs official. "Stage fright."

Mitch Cantrell could not have gotten to the top of his profession without having a built-in lie detector. At that moment, the needle was going right off the scale.

"Sure." His own smile was every bit as dazzling—and as false—as hers had been. "You go take your bath, Tory, while I call room service. Then later, you and I can have a nice long talk."

"I don't suppose that you'd be willing to back off on this one, would you, Mitch?" Tory asked suddenly.

"Nope."

"Even if I promise you an exclusive?"

He lifted a brow. "If the story's hot enough for you to go to this much trouble, why wouldn't you want to write about it?"

Exhaustion and the stress of the last few weeks made her temper flare. "Because it's more than just a story, dammit. It's personal. And I'd like to keep it that way."

Mitch rubbed his square jaw and studied her silently. For a fleeting moment, Tory allowed herself to think that he actually would turn away and walk out the door, leaving her to do what she'd come all these miles to do.

"Sorry," he said, dashing her hopes. "I've seen that look in those gorgeous eyes before, Victoria. Usually right before you landed yourself in some very hot and choppy waters. No, as much as I hate to decline a lady's offer, I'm going to have to stick around and make certain that you don't get that lovely, albeit blindingly bright blond head blown off."

"Dammit, Mitch—"

"You'd better hurry," he reminded her, casting a significant glance at his watch. "After all, it wouldn't do for La Rubia to show up late for her command performance before General Ramirez."

Realizing the futility of arguing further, Tory stomped out of the room, vowing to think of something—anything—to keep Mitch from ruining her plans.

2

TORY STAYED in the bathtub long after the fragrant bubbles had dissolved and the water cooled. Although she knew it was cowardly, she wanted to put off the confrontation with Mitch for as long as she could. The only problem was, she knew that if she kept him waiting too long, he'd simply come to her.

Little things like protocol and social amenities had never proven any obstacle to Mitch when he was on the scent of a story. He wouldn't hesitate to invade the privacy of her bathroom, and the idea of being alone, naked, with him in such close proximity, was more unsettling than facing the barrage of questions she knew would be awaiting her.

She couldn't tell him the truth. Tory had no doubt that if Mitch had even an inkling of what she was planning to do, he'd hit the roof. Then he'd do whatever it took to stop her.

Her mind drifted to her sister. Had it only been six weeks since she'd received Amy's letter while working in Lithuania? The moment her landlady had handed her the thin airmail envelope, Tory had been struck with a feeling of impending disaster. That feeling had escalated when she read the letter.

The fact that her younger sister was having an affair was nothing new; Amy had always been a beautiful butterfly, flitting from man to man in a never-ending search for love. She had never known their father; he'd deserted the family shortly after her birth. Which explained, Tory had decided long ago, why the men in her sister's life were always nearly twenty years older. They were also, unfortunately, the type of men who were incapable of commitment.

After dropping out of college, Amy had drifted for a while, then joined the USO tour and begun singing to troops at American bases around the world. It had been at the U.S. army base in La Paz that she had met General José Enrique Ramirez. Enthralled, she'd left the tour and remained in the country, singing at the Hotel de la Revolución.

This time Amy had gotten herself into more trouble than she understood. Having an affair with the married general was dangerous enough. What was insane was that she had concocted a plan to make him divorce his wife and marry her. He was up to something illegal, Amy had written in her last letter. All she had to do was find out what and confront him with her knowledge.

It was blackmail, pure and simple, but the way Amy described her intended actions, she was merely "putting a little fire under the general to get him to do what he really wants to do, anyway."

The first thing Tory had done after reading the letter was check the postmark. Unsurprisingly, it had taken ten weeks for the letter to get from Playa de Palma, La Paz, to Vilnius, Lithuania. Weeks that for her sister had proved nearly fatal.

While Tory tried frantically to get through the maze that was the Lithuanian phone system, Amy was struck by a hit-and-run driver as she left the Playa de Palma hotel after her midnight show. Her injuries would force her to spend at least six months in the Miami hospital she had been flown to, more if she opted for the plastic surgery needed to restore her once-exquisite face.

The police had not been able to apprehend the driver. The hour had been late, the night dark, the streets nearly deserted. There were no witnesses. While the official report apparently satisfied the American ambassador to La Paz, Tory hadn't believed it for a minute. Unfortunately, Amy's concussion had left a large gap in her memory.

All she wanted to do, Amy had complained when Tory arrived at the Miami hospital, was get better so that she could get on with her life. Not that she was going to have much of a life looking like this, she'd lamented, sobbing dramatically every time she glanced into the mirror.

Looking at her sister's shattered face, broken body and sensing her wounded spirit, the idea of revenge was sparked. It flickered in the back of Tory's mind for days, building slowly, relentlessly, until it consumed all her other emotions. Even her common sense.

Determined to uncover and then reveal the truth, she had to find a way to get close to the general. It was then she'd conceived the plan to create a false identity for herself, an identity as a sexy blond cabaret singer. A woman the general would not be able to resist. A woman like Amy.

Although Tory still wasn't certain how she was going to pull off her admittedly risky scheme, she did know that she wasn't going to accomplish anything hiding in the bathroom.

Heaving a sigh, she rose from the still-perfumed tepid water, dried herself with the bath towel and dressed in a pair of jeans and T-shirt. At first she was tempted to do something with her hair and touch up her makeup. Then, determined not to let Mitch think she was primping on his account, she marched defiantly from the bathroom.

He was standing in front of the window, her dark blue passport in his hand.

"What are you doing? Going through my private papers?" she demanded furiously. She'd known him to be unscrupulous when he was on the trail of a story, but had never thought he'd stoop to snooping through a colleague's purse!

Mitch ignored her obvious anger. "Where the hell did you come up with a name like Pandora Cavanaugh?"

She crossed the room and snatched the passport from his hand. "Whatever name I choose is none of your damn business. Why don't you just go find a war zone and leave me alone?"

"I've got another idea."

She crossed her arms over her chest. "Now why doesn't that surprise me?"

Her sarcasm, like her anger, appeared to roll right off his back. "Why don't we discuss your newly discovered penchant for disguises and forged papers over dinner?"

He gestured toward the round table set on the terrace, overlooking the cerulean waters of the Caribbean Sea. On the linen-draped table were a flickering candle in a hurricane glass, a bottle of red wine and an assortment of covered plates. The rich, unmistakable aroma stopped her in her tracks.

"Is that what I think it is?"

Mitch turned toward her, experiencing a quick, unexpected sexual tug as he noticed how nicely the jeans hugged her hips and the appealing way in which the red cotton T-shirt clung to the soft swell of her breasts. She'd discarded the vivid green contacts, returning her eyes to the soft, doe-brown color that he remembered so fondly. Her hair was piled high atop her head, anchored with what appeared to be a pair of ebony chopsticks.

Mitch was vastly relieved to discover that the brassy blond hair had been a wig. A few brunette tendrils had escaped to curl wetly down the side of her neck and he had a sudden, irrational need to twist one of those damp curls around his fingers.

Suppressing the sexual urge, he moved to the table and lifted the stainless steel cover on one of the plates. "A bacon cheeseburger for milady," he announced with a pleased grin. "And French fries. And a banana split for dessert. With extra nuts."

Damn the man! He had the memory of an elephant. Even she had almost forgotten their conversation that first night they'd spent together, when they'd been hunkered down in a cave, caught in the cross fire between rebel and government forces. When it had seemed that there would be no escape, she had complained that it wasn't fair that she was going to die without having an opportunity for a last meal.

Mitch, appearing undaunted by the shelling, had asked her what she'd choose. Her answer had been instantaneous: bacon cheeseburgers, French fries and a banana split. With extra nuts.

"You'll never change, will you?" she asked now.

Mitch frowned. That was the same thing Allie had said, right before she told him she was marrying another man. "I guess not. Is that so bad?"

If Tory hadn't been watching him so closely, she would have missed the flash of vulnerability in his eyes. How strange. She'd always considered Mitch Cantrell to be the most confident man in the world. To discover that he might be mortal, after all, was a revelation.

"Probably not," she answered carefully. Her sharp eyes took in his rigid shoulders, his uncommonly stiff stance. There were undercurrents swirling between them that she could not quite get a handle on. "At least you haven't lost your knack for grand gestures."

"Is that good?"

"Of course." She looked at him curiously. What woman wouldn't love to know that there was a man somewhere in the world who'd remember her every wish? Even eight years later.

"I've been told that some women respond better to little, everyday things."

Some women? Like his wife? Tory wondered. "Well, I for one am grateful for a bacon cheeseburger anytime I can get it," she said, attempting to lighten the suddenly too serious mood. "Especially after months of Lithuanian food."

As he opened the bottle of wine, Mitch appreciated the way she'd deftly changed the subject. The Tory he remembered would have grabbed hold of his momentary lack of assurance, gnawing at it like a terrier with a bone, refusing to let go until he'd spilled all his secrets. Something he was not yet prepared to do.

The constant pain that had accompanied the breakup of his marriage had eased over the past months to a low, dull ache. But he wasn't ready to talk about it. Especially to the only other woman he'd ever considered spending a lifetime with.

"That's one place I've never been," he said, pulling out a chair. "I take it Lithuanian fare is not exactly haute cuisine?"

"Hardly," Tory answered as she sat down. When the aroma of the cheeseburger wafted up from the gold-rimmed plate, she realized that she was starving. "In fact, if I never see another piece of black bread or sausage or herring, it'll be too soon." She bit into the cheeseburger, discovering that it tasted every bit as delicious as it smelled.

Mitch cut into his steak. It was tough, but tasty. "Herring?"

Tory bit into a French fry. It was perfect—golden and crisp on the outside, tender on the inside. "They catch herring from the Baltic," she explained when she finished chewing. "This is heavenly. I owe you one, Cantrell."

This time his smile was genuine. "That's the idea."

A congenial silence settled over the table as they ate. The tangerine sun sank into the sea, turning the water a deep, burnished copper. Below them, a pair of lovers strolled on the hard-packed sand, arms wrapped around one another, stopping every few feet to exchange kisses.

Tory knew that she should be angry at Mitch for manipulating her this way, but had to admit that were the shoe on the other foot, she'd do the same thing. How many times had she used similar tactics to soften up a source? Too many to count.

"I'll make you a deal."

Pushing his plate aside, Mitch leaned back in his chair and observed her carefully over the crystal rim of his wineglass. "What kind of deal?"

"I'll tell you what I'm doing here in La Paz if you promise to leave me alone to do it."

He shook his head. "You know I can't agree to that, Tory."

Her temper flared again. "Dammit, Mitch, this doesn't have anything to do with you."

"The hell it doesn't," he grunted. "Because anything that involves you damn well involves me, Victoria Elizabeth Martin!"

Mitch was as surprised to have said the words as Tory was to hear them. For a long drawn-out moment they stared at one another over the table. Old feelings stirred, memories of long ago tugged at familiar sensual chords. The sea breeze blew the loose strand of hair against her cheek; Mitch's fingers practically itched with the urge to brush it away.

"What does that mean?" Tory finally asked. Below them she could hear the soft sigh of the tide lapping against the white sugar sand.

Mitch didn't take his eyes from hers. "I'm not sure. But I do know that if you've come down here dressed up like a cross between Marilyn Monroe and Cher to make a play for Ramirez, you are playing with fire, lady. And we go back too far for me to sit by on the sidelines and let you self-destruct."

Tory might have taken his words at face value, if it hadn't been for the lambent flame burning in the depths of his eyes. He'd looked at her that way before. Right before they'd made love for the first time.

"So what are you doing down here?" she asked, moving the subject to neutral ground. "I thought you were in Colombia."

"Things got a little hot down there," he said blandly.

"The same old Mitch," she said with a smile that was both wry and fond at the same time. "The master of the understatement. I saw your exposé on the drug cartel the day I got back to the States and am amazed that you're still alive."

"The network, along with the Colombian government, seem to share your concern. That's why they thought it might be a good idea if I came here and covered the elections. Such as they are." He didn't mention that he was currently chasing rumors that, if true, could put an end to the general's military rule.

Tory knew that even with another week to go, all the polls were declaring General Ramirez the winner. Which wasn't surprising, since he'd reportedly threatened any citizen who might be foolish enough to vote for his opponent Elena Castillo, the widow of the former publisher of *La Libertad*. Three years ago, after writing a scathing editorial, Juan Castillo had been killed, reportedly by an armed robber. So the general's threat, along with several thousand phony ballots allegedly stored at government headquarters, made the entire election a farce.

"You believe Ramirez is going to win?" she asked.

"There's unspoken support for Castillo, but I don't know if it'll manifest itself at the polls."

"You haven't heard any rumors about illegalities?"

Mitch shrugged. "Election illegalities are standard operating procedure in La Paz."

"I wasn't talking about election fraud. I was wondering if you'd run across anything else?"

Mitch kept his expression inscrutable. "Such as?"

It was Tory's turn to shrug. "I don't know. Drugs perhaps?"

"Not on a bet. Hell, Tory, the penalty for being caught selling dope down here is tougher than it is in Singapore."

"I know that. I just thought perhaps..." Her voice drifted off. She knew Ramirez was up to something. Something so sinister her sister had nearly died to keep his secret.

"Perhaps what?"

"General Ramirez is far from a Boy Scout," Tory observed. "I just thought that if some of his less than admirable activities became well-known, it might have an impact on the election."

"I suppose that would depend on exactly what activities you're referring to," Mitch began, wondering what, if anything, Tory knew. "And I suppose this is where I remind you that I don't like playing games, Tory. If you're trying to get off the hook by changing the subject, you're making a big mistake."

"That wasn't at all what I was trying to do," Tory said, not quite truthfully. Actually she was interested in everything about the general.

"Why don't you just come clean about what you're up to?"

"There's nothing to come clean about," she insisted. "You know that I once considered becoming a professional singer."

"I remember you sang with a high school rock band," Mitch agreed. She'd also brought the house down with a sexy torch song for the press corps Follies during La Paz's raucous carnival.

"Well, I kept wondering if I could have made a career for myself."

"You have a career," Mitch felt obliged to point out. "One you're damn good at."

Tory tried to ignore the burst of pleasure his words aroused. She'd discovered early in their relationship that although Mitch would compliment a woman on such feminine attributes as hair or clothing, he was incredibly stingy when it came to handing out accolades for journalistic endeavors.

Not that he wasn't equally as demanding of himself. Was it *Time* or *Newsweek* that had stated that Mitchell Cantrell brought an unparalleled depth to electronic journalism? Whichever, Tory remembered that the magazine had also declared he had a genius for discovering the single nugget of truth hidden beneath a mountain of political manure.

So why was she even trying to lie to him? she asked herself. The answer was simple: she had no choice.

"I was referring to a career in show business," she responded.

"You want show business, come into television," he suggested. "The medium is in desperate need of brilliant writers and as a decided bonus, you're gorgeous enough to satisfy those idiot executives who spend all their time pacing the oriental carpets in their ivory towers, worrying about ratings."

Now she was not only damn good, he was actually calling her brilliant! Would wonders never cease? "I suppose I should take that as a compliment," Tory remarked, "since there was a time when you didn't believe I could write my byline without screwing up."

"I never said that," Mitch argued. "I simply said that you had a great deal to learn."

She'd been three years out of Northwestern when she left the relative safety and anonymity of the political beat on the Cleveland *Plain Dealer* to take a job with the Associated Press. Her first foreign assignment had been the civil war in La Paz. Thinking back on her arrival in the city, clad in a pair of designer jeans, a pair of fawn-colored Italian suede boots and a khaki safari shirt from Banana Republic, Tory blushed.

"You were a good teacher," she allowed.

Mitch knew that he'd been damn hard on her. But it had been for her own good. From her first article about the refugees fleeing into the neighboring countries, she'd proven she had a great, albeit raw talent. Unfortunately her survival skills had been practically nonexistent, and whatever interview tactics she'd picked up chasing down Ohio political scandals just didn't cut it in a war zone.

"You're a smart lady. I didn't teach you anything you wouldn't have picked up by yourself eventually."

"If I'd stayed alive long enough."

He chuckled at that. "You were a bit of a loose cannon, all right." And Mitch had a feeling she still was, whatever stunt she was trying to pull off this time.

Tory welcomed this little detour down memory lane, hoping it would keep him from probing into her reason for being here in La Paz. It didn't.

"What are you up to, Tory?" he asked quietly. Firmly.

"I really am here to sing, Mitch." That much at least was the truth.

"Even if I believed that, which I don't," he told her, "why the phony papers?"

"Simple. As you've already pointed out, I do have a career. One in which I'm asking people to take me seriously. I was afraid that if I fell on my face, it would damage my credibility with my readers."

"So that's why you concocted this La Rubia act?"

He wasn't buying a word of it. "That's the reason," she lied blithely.

"I have to give you credit for dynamite advance publicity," Mitch allowed. "How the hell did you pull that off?"

"I picked up the phony passport in Hong Kong," Tory admitted. "The posters were easy, but I owe the advance publicity and the booking to a friend at the embassy."

"Anyone I know?"

"Jerry Maxwell. We dated for a short time while we were both posted to Panama."

"Maxwell," Mitch mused. "Tall guy, built like a Coke machine?"

"He works out." Tory heard the sarcasm in Mitch's tone and wondered if he could possibly be jealous. "Actually Jerry made a terrific press agent. Unfortunately he was transferred to Peru last week, so I'm on my own." Tory didn't mention how much Jerry's unexpected departure had upset her.

Mitch was not sorry to have the guy out of Tory's life. He was too smooth, too good-looking in a muscle-bound sort of way.

"So what do the AP honchos think about your career move?"

"They don't know."

Mitch narrowed his eyes. "Give me a break, Tory."

"I put in for a three-week vacation. They think I'm lying on the beach in Maui. Really," she insisted, reading his disbelieving expression. "You can call the office and check."

"I just might do that. So tell me something else."

"What?" She was beginning to understand why his interview subjects began to squirm after the first couple of questions.

"What makes you think you can get away without anyone—especially one of your former colleagues—recognizing you?"

Good question. One she'd debated for weeks. Until she'd looked into the mirror after her make-over at André Géricault's famed Fifth Avenue salon. "I'm a print reporter, so my face isn't well-known like you TV guys. Also, most of the correspondents who were covering La Paz eight years ago have given up traveling and are happily ensconced behind local anchor desks or working in D.C."

"I'm still here," Mitch pointed out.

"You're different. You'll be running off to cover the world's hot spots on your hundredth birthday."

Mitch could certainly think of worse ways to spend his old age. "Still, with so many people down here covering the election, there's a chance of running into someone you've met."

"Everyone's too busy trying to uncover election fraud to pay any attention to a hotel lounge singer," she argued. "And even if there was a reason to suspect La Rubia's credentials, which there isn't, I think I've done a pretty good job of changing my appearance."

"I recognized you right away."

She lowered her gaze and began tracing small circles on the tablecloth with a ruby fingernail. "But you know me better than any of the others. What we had was . . . different."

More intimate, she meant.

Watching the soft color drift into her cheeks, Mitch felt another low, deep pull of desire. "I'm glad to hear that I wasn't just a wartime fling."

The color deepened, reminding Mitch of the bloom of late-summer roses in his mother's San Francisco garden. "You know better than that," she told him softly.

"Yes." His eyes fixed on her face. "I think I do."

Deciding that it was time to close the subject, Tory scooped up a spoonful of chocolate sauce from her banana split. "Mmm," she said, following it with a blissful sigh that was entirely feigned. "This really is delicious."

Mitch frowned as he poured the rich café au lait from the silver pot into their cups. He was growing more and more frustrated. It was obvious that Tory was lying through her lovely white teeth. It was also plain that he could keep her in this suite for as long as it took to wring the truth from her. He was, after all, bigger and a great deal stronger. And if he had an aversion to using physical force, all he had to do was pick up the phone, call immigration and mention the little matter of a forged passport and she'd be back on the next plane to the States. Out of harm's way.

But something in her eyes told him that both actions would be a mistake. Victoria Martin was the most intransigent woman he'd ever met. She took orders about as well as he did and he knew that the more he pushed, the more she'd take off in the other direction. And probably end up getting herself killed into the bargain.

That being the case, he had no choice but to play this game by her rules. For now.

Tory knew Mitch well enough to know that she was eventually going to have to throw in the towel. He'd be bound to find out everything. And when he did, she knew that the resultant explosion would register off the Richter scale. But for now she was determined to keep the truth from him as long as she could. At least until after this evening's performance.

The atmosphere between them had become too charged for comfort. What Tory couldn't decide was whether all the latent energy was due to the scent of a hot story or to lingering sexual memories. If she was to be perfectly honest with herself, she would have to admit that though she intended to bring down the general, she also possessed a healthy fear about her ability to succeed.

Mitch stared out over the water, thinking back to the stir caused by Tory's arrival in La Paz eight years ago. The word among the press corps had been that the new correspondent was smart, aggressive and undeniably gorgeous. Unfortunately she only got excited about one thing, one rebuffed male complained. And that was seeing her byline in print. As for sex, rumors were that the AP might as well have signed on a Carmelite nun. Because Victoria Martin saved whatever passion lurked inside that cover-girl exterior solely for her work.

Until the night she and Mitch became separated from the rebel patrol they were covering and were forced to seek shelter in a cave while rockets screamed overhead. The battle raged for forty-eight hours, during which time Tory displayed a deep-seated passion that had nothing to do with journalism. Their turbulent affair had continued for three months.

Once, one of them, he couldn't remember whom, had casually brought up marriage. They'd both immediately agreed that although it was an admirable institution, they had no desire to spend the rest of their life there. It had become their private joke and if the humor grew a little hollow as the weeks went by, neither Mitch nor Tory admitted it.

They were two free souls, she'd insisted. Thrown together for this brief, inflammatory time. They were too alike, Mitch had answered on cue. They were both competitive, driven and far too restless to ever settle down. So when the time came to go their separate ways, each pretended not to care. Periodically Mitch would read one of Tory's riveting AP stories and wonder what would have happened if he'd actually asked her to stay with him. But then he would never have married Allie.

Tory's soft words shattered his introspection, proving that they were on the same wavelength. "I saw your wife on television," she ventured cautiously. After Mitch's abduction, Alanna Cantrell had become an outspoken spokesperson for the hostage families. She'd been a frequent guest on television talk shows for years, refusing to allow Americans to forget their captive countrymen. "She's a beautiful, articulate woman."

"She is that." Mitch waited for the hurt, both relieved and a little surprised when it didn't come. "I'd known Allie for years. One June I returned home for my dad's funeral and discovered that the girl next door had grown up during my absence. Since I had to get right back to Beirut, we were married a week later."

"You never were one to let any grass grow under your feet once you'd set your mind to something." Tory felt a faint stab of something that resembled jealousy. Or regret. She ignored it. "If you ever tell anyone that I said this, I'll deny it to my dying day, but there isn't a woman alive anywhere in the world who doesn't fantasize about being swept off her feet. Your wife is a lucky woman."

"Former wife," Mitch said, so quietly that Tory almost thought she'd imagined it.

"Oh, Mitch." She took his hand and linked their fingers.

"Apparently when the State Department declared me dead, they effectively put an end to our marriage," he explained. "That by itself probably wouldn't have created a problem, if the Islamic jihad hadn't had such lousy timing."

"What do you mean?"

"They released me right before Alanna's wedding to the guy who was remodeling her house. It's a vintage San Francisco Victorian," he said. "Apparently it was a wreck when she bought it. You should see what she— what they've done to it."

"I'm sure it's lovely," she said dryly. "Are you telling me that she chose an old house . . . and some carpenter over you?"

Her incredulous expression did wonders for his self-esteem. "He's not just a carpenter," Mitch felt obliged to point out. "Actually, Jonas Harte is quite a successful architect. And as much as I hate to admit it, he'll probably make a better husband than I ever could have been."

"I doubt that," Tory muttered, thinking that Alanna Cantrell had always seemed such an intelligent woman. Obviously appearances were deceptive.

"Really he will." Mitch found it odd to be in a position of defending his former rival. "Jonas is bedrock solid, the kind of guy to put down deep roots. He wants kids, which is something Allie and I never could agree on, and he'll undoubtedly be able to build a better tree house than I ever could."

Tory had always felt that roots were something that kept you tied to one place. "He sounds boring," she commented.

"Different strokes," Mitch murmured as he leaned toward her. Idly he curled a loose strand of hair around his finger, pleased to find that it was still as soft as silk. Although she'd always worn her hair in a braid while working, alone at night she had left it loose. He loved getting lost in that hair. Drowning in it.

His fingers brushed her collarbone, creating feelings that were both exciting and frightening at the same time. He could hurt her again, Tory realized. Oh, he wouldn't mean to, but he would. And this time she wasn't certain she would have the strength to recover. She had to back away from this. Now, while she still could.

She took a deep breath. "As much as I'd love to stay here and chat about old times, it's getting late. I really have to get ready for my performance," she said in a calm voice that was not as steady as she would have liked.

Anger flared; Mitch pushed it down. "We have to talk."

Tory was no fool. She knew that as soon as Mitch heard what she was about to undertake, he would do whatever it took to stop her. And that was one thing she could not—would not—allow.

"After my performance," she hedged.

His eyes never left hers. "What time is your last set?"

Instead of feeling relieved at his seeming surrender, Tory reacted warily. "Eleven."

"Fine." He nodded. "I'll meet you in your dressing room. Then we can come back here and settle things."

If everything went as planned, she wouldn't be coming back to her room at all. Instead she would be going home with General José Enrique Ramirez. And she'd like to see Mitch try and stop that.

Her acquiescent smile belied the runaway pounding of her heart. "Whatever you say, Mitch," she agreed sweetly.

Mitch had explored every inch of Tory's firm body; he'd tasted her warm flesh, discovered that sensitive spot behind her knee where she liked to be kissed, and knew that she had a birthmark shaped like a half moon right below her left breast.

He knew that she'd had chicken pox when she was seven, had spent her junior and senior years of high school singing the lead in a female rock band. After graduating, she'd studied at Northwestern University's acclaimed school of journalism, where she'd lost her virginity in her junior year to a business major, the night of Tau Kappa Epsilon's spring fling.

Her taste in music was remarkably eclectic, ranging from Mozart and Beethoven to Muddy Waters' blues and from Billy Joel and Alice Cooper to Waylon Jennings. Her favorite books were John F. Kennedy's *Pro-*

files in Courage and Tolstoy's *Anna Karenina*, which she reread religiously once a year, even though she thought Anna was a damn fool to throw herself under the train.

Tory's favorite color was red, her favorite foods were bacon cheeseburgers and fries, and her childhood dream had been to be a fireman. Or a race-car driver. Or Janis Joplin.

He'd thought he knew everything there was to know about Tory Martin.

But as he looked once more into her uplifted face, Mitch realized he'd never known what an adept liar she could be.

3

HER DRESSING ROOM was filled with flowers. One elaborate arrangement of gladioli and peach blossoms was from the management of the hotel. A dazzling creation of bird-of-paradise flowers and giant poppies was from the American ambassador. The remainder—baskets and baskets of brilliant blossoms—were from General Ramirez, along with a bottle of French champagne and an iced silver bowl of caviar.

Unaccustomed to wearing makeup, Tory struggled with the myriad pencils, pots of gleaming color and brushes that André had assured her she needed to duplicate his dazzling artistry. When the makeup artist had demonstrated how to smudge the pewter-gray eye shadow with her thumb, the result had been smoldering sex appeal. Now, although Tory tried to follow his instructions to the letter, all she succeeded in doing was making herself look like the bride of Dracula. Sighing, she reached for the cold cream and a tissue and decided to try again.

Finally she put down the gray kohl pencil and judiciously studied herself in the mirror. That was definitely better. She looked good. Better than good. She looked sexy. As she bent her head and inserted the contact lenses that changed her eyes from a soft brown to a gleaming emerald, Tory hoped that the general would find her sexy.

She'd just zipped up the red-beaded dress when there was a knock on her dressing-room door. "Come in," she called.

The door opened to a woman carrying a breathtaking bouquet of blue moon orchids and amaryllis. "Don't tell me," Tory said.

"They are from General Ramirez," the woman confirmed.

"The general must own an interest in a chain of flower shops."

The dry remark flew right over the woman's head. "Oh, no. It is simply that he finds you very lovely, La Rubia."

"I'm beginning to get that idea," Tory agreed, "since he's written the same thing on every card." The flowers' perfume was so overwhelming that she was beginning to get a headache.

"Would you please have someone send all these to the local hospitals after my performance?"

The woman's eyes widened. "But, La Rubia, the general—"

Tory cut her off with an impatient wave of her hand. "What the general doesn't know won't hurt him. Besides, he gave the flowers to me. So they are mine to dispose of as I wish."

"But—"

Tory read the fear in the other woman's eyes. "Don't worry. I'll take the blame if the general is displeased."

The woman nodded obediently, but her expression failed to display confidence. Tory wondered if this woman had known her sister. She wanted to ask if Amy had been happy singing here. Had she enjoyed the flowers, the champagne, the caviar?

But knowing the folly of taking a chance that the general might find out that La Rubia was asking about an unknown accident victim, Tory held her tongue. Instead she left the dressing room and made her way backstage.

The piano player had just finished Gershwin's "They Can't Take That Away from Me." The audience was anxious for her appearance. Tory could hear the chanting: "La Rubia, La Rubia!" When the stage manager introduced her, she walked into the blinding white light to the sound of cheers.

Mitch sat at the rosewood bar, watching the red bugle beads shimmer as Tory moved across the stage to the microphone. Her hair glistened in the spotlight like molten gold and the flesh revealed by the strapless gown gleamed like fine porcelain. A hush fell over the room as she took the microphone from its stand and held it between her palms. When she smiled there was an audible sigh from the men in the audience.

She'd chosen a blues medley for her first set. The songs were slow and sultry, bringing to mind steamy summer evenings on New Orleans's famed Bourbon Street. She started out with Billy Holiday's "Billie's Blues," segueing smoothly into "Good Morning, Heartache," then "He Made a Woman out of Me." She was getting into the feel of the music, swaying in a way clearly designed to arouse erotic fantasies in the most sober-minded of men.

The strapless red dress hugged her curves like a lover's caress and when she moved, the slits in the gown parted, revealing her long legs, her smooth, firm thighs. The general, Mitch noticed, was leaning forward, his dark eyes drinking in the sight.

Mitch reminded himself that it was Tory up on that stage. Tory of the quick temper and even quicker wit. She wasn't really La Rubia at all, but Victoria Martin, the aggressive, headstrong AP reporter. But when she started in on "Can't Help Lovin' That Man," her smoky voice wringing more from the lyrics than Mitch could have imagined possible, he began to ache with a deep visceral hunger.

Long-dormant emotions stirred, needs flared. Mitch had a sudden urge to jump onto the stage, fling La Rubia over his shoulder and carry her off caveman-style to the nearest bed.

There was a long drawn-out moment of silence after she allowed the final note to drift away. Then the applause began, slowly at first, as if the audience were waking from a particularly sensual dream, then growing louder and louder until the cheers and clapping reached deafening proportions.

Tory held up a hand. At her silent command the applause stopped. Heady with her heretofore unknown power, she took a deep breath then directed her gaze to the general's table.

"*¡Gracias!*" she said in a low voice that was as warm and as smooth as silk. She continued in fluent Spanish, to the delight of all present. "You've been so kind. I do hope you'll stay for my second set." The invitation was issued to the room, but her eyes remained on the general. Then, flashing her dazzling smile, she disappeared into the shadows.

Tory began counting as soon as she reached her dressing room. Before she'd reached thirty there was a knock at the door. "Come in."

Her visitor was a young soldier in his midtwenties. From his uniform she took him to be a member of the general's hated military police. From his swagger she knew he was proud of the ribbons adorning the front of that uniform. Viewing the naked cruelty in his eyes, Tory had a disconcerting flash of how he'd earned those ribbons.

"May I help you?" She sat down at her dressing table and began to repair her makeup.

It was obvious that the man did not appreciate being treated with such overt disregard. His dark eyes narrowed dangerously. "General José Enrique Ramirez requests your company at a late supper after your performance."

Dipping her finger into a small round pot, Tory proceeded to rub rosy cream blush into her cheekbones. "I'm flattered," she said. "However, I'm afraid I'm unable to attend."

The officer stiffened. "Perhaps you do not understand."

"On the contrary." Tory flashed him a smile in the mirror. "I understand perfectly. However, the general must understand that La Rubia does not accept invitations from underlings."

For a long, dangerous moment their eyes met and held. Hatred glittered in the depths of his dark brown eyes. Inwardly shaking, Tory held her ground, relying on her ability to remain outwardly calm.

"I will give the general your message," he said.

Tory nodded. "Please do."

The soldier turned abruptly on his heel and stomped out of the dressing room, slamming the door behind him. Then, and only then, did Tory begin breathing again.

"Nice bluff. What did you intend to do if he called you on it?"

She spun around, staring at Mitch, who'd come from behind her dressing screen. "What are you doing here?"

"Keeping an eye on you," he said easily. "You realize, of course, that goon would just as soon rape you as look at you."

True. She'd seen it in the man's eyes during that suspended moment in the mirror. "Not so long as his boss is interested in La Rubia."

"Ah, but what about when the general's interest wanes?" Mitch countered. "Have you thought about that?"

Tory wondered what Mitch would say if she were to tell him that she knew better than anyone what happened to a woman who fell out of General Ramirez's favor.

"I thought I'd take one thing at a time," she said with feigned equilibrium.

She was a damned good actress, Mitch allowed. Better than he would have imagined. But he knew he hadn't imagined the way she'd paled at his question and wondered yet again just what Tory was up to.

"At least you're admitting that there's more to this than a mere singing audition."

She frowned. "That wasn't what I said at all."

Mitch looked inclined to answer when there was another knock at the door. This one harsher, more deliberate than the first.

"You have to get out of here," Tory whispered furiously, gesturing toward the window.

Mitch shook his head and slipped back behind the screen. Damning him for being so stubborn, Tory took a deep breath that was meant to calm, but didn't, and called out, "*¿Sí?*"

The general didn't wait for an invitation. He entered the dressing room, a white rose in his hand. "For La Rubia," he said, extending the rose. "From her most humble admirer, General José Enrique Ramirez." From the exaggerated way he announced his name, Tory half expected to hear a flourish of trumpets.

She smiled. "That's very nice of you, *señor general*, but my goodness, you've already sent so many exquisite bouquets. I wouldn't be at all surprised to learn that there are no flowers left blooming anywhere in the country."

"One of La Paz's major exports, along with its coffee, fruit and tobacco, is its wide variety of flowers. Yet nowhere in our entire country is there a blossom as exquisite as La Rubia."

His deep voice was a velvet embrace. His eyes were warm as his lips curved beneath the black mustache. A foolish or vulnerable woman could easily drown in those dark warm depths. For the first time Tory understood how her sister could have fallen prey to this evil man.

She lowered her gaze so he could not see the hatred she was feeling. "You flatter me, *señor general.*"

"I merely speak the truth," he insisted smoothly. "Corporal Fuentes told me that you turned down my invitation."

Tory lifted her eyes to his. "I turned down the corporal's invitation," she corrected.

"I am not accustomed to approaching women myself."

She tossed her head in the way Rita Hayworth had made famous in *Gilda*. After watching the movie on the late show last week, Tory had practiced the provocative gesture in front of her mirror. "And I am not accustomed to being treated like a woman who could be hired for the evening."

He arched a black brow as if to disagree. "I never thought of you as a prostitute."

She heard the sound of the keyboard as the pianist began his final set. "Then you should have instructed your corporal not to treat me like one." Turning away, she laid down the rose upon her dressing table and returned to the task of repairing her makeup.

Obviously irritated, the general put his hand on her shoulder. "It appears we have a misunderstanding."

Loath to have this man touch her, Tory was about to shrug off his hand, then decided that she'd pushed the general far enough. For now. "Perhaps we do," she allowed.

His fingers stroked her neck. "Would it make a difference if I were to invite you to this late-night supper myself?"

Although his touch was making her skin crawl, Tory managed to conceal her distaste. "It might."

Frustration flashed in his eyes, but the general's tone remained studiously polite. "It would give me great pleasure if La Rubia would dine with me in her hotel suite after her performance tonight."

She was halfway there. Forcing down her nerves, Tory turned and gave him her sweetest smile. "I would love to dine with you, *señor general*." Before he could answer, she added, "But not at my hotel, where anyone can interrupt us."

"Then where?" he snapped. It was obvious that his infamous temper was reaching the breaking point.

"I think we should dine at your house." She held her breath, awaiting the impending explosion.

The general gave her a long, hard look. Finally he appeared to make his decision. "My wife is in the country," he said, not telling Tory anything she didn't know. "I'll instruct my housekeeper to prepare a room for you." His hands caressed her shoulders, her arms. When they approached her breasts, Tory intervened.

"I'd like that. Very much," she lied, her green eyes offering him a sensual promise. "But now, if you don't mind, General Ramirez, I must prepare for my second set." She rose from the dressing table and he took a long, slow tour of her, from the top of her golden head to the feet clad in skyscraper-stiletto heels.

"I await tonight with eager anticipation," the general said. Matters apparently settled to his satisfaction, he lifted her hand to his lips, then left the dressing room.

"Okay, that's it," Mitch announced, coming from behind the screen again. "Either you get on a plane back to the States right now, or I'm turning you in to immigration."

Anger washed away the fear the general had left behind. "You wouldn't dare!"

Mitch crossed his arms over his chest and glared at her. "It's either that or having me tie you up, stuffing you into a duffel bag and tossing you in the back of a military cargo plane."

"I'd like to see you try it!"

"Actually, now I give the matter some thought, that last choice does sound like the most fun. I don't suppose you have any rope handy?"

"Of course not," Tory snapped.

Mitch glanced around the room. "No problem." Plucking a pair of black stockings from a nearby chair, he moved toward her, his eyes darkening to the dangerous hue of a storm-tossed sea. "We can use these."

"Dammit, Mitch." Tory snatched the stockings out of his hand and flung them onto the floor. "Why can't you leave me alone?"

"Because you have no idea what you're doing."

"Now that's where you're wrong," she insisted quietly. Firmly. "I know exactly what I'm doing."

How could he have forgotten how stubborn she was? It was a good thing they hadn't gotten married, Mitch decided furiously. The woman would have driven him to drink before the honeymoon was over.

"You're not leaving this room until you tell me what this is all about," he said in a low voice that Tory knew was more dangerous than the loudest shout.

"I'm sorry, but I really can't tell you," she insisted. "Not yet."

Mitch felt the fresh surge of fury and welcomed it. Ever since the breakup of his marriage he'd simply been going through the motions. How long had it been since he'd felt anything? Too long. "Dammit, Victoria, you're behaving like some character in a paperback thriller. This is real life, lady. So knock off the 'spy vs spy' routine. Before you end up getting yourself killed!"

He was looming over her, forcing her to tilt her head back in order to see his eyes. He was angry. More than angry. He was as furious as she'd ever seen him.

She threw up her chin, meeting his blistering glare with a furious look of her own. "Leave me alone."

Frustrated, he curved his fingers around her naked shoulders, as if to shake some sense into that gorgeous blond head. But then their eyes met and the passion born of shared anger turned to something else.

"No," she whispered.

He pulled her closer. "I think it's time you learned that you can't call all the shots."

"If you're trying to frighten me, it isn't going to work," Tory insisted. "You forget that I know you. Well enough to know that you're not the kind of man who'd force himself on a woman against her will."

"That's true." His fingers skimmed her back, releasing a sensation of excitement on the delicate bones of her spine. "But we both know that I won't have to use force, Victoria."

Her knees were turning to water, her blood hummed thickly in her veins. But Tory was too much of a fighter to surrender to his arrogant statement. "Now there's where you're wrong."

With a cool hard glare she dared him to make his move.

He did. Before she could evade him, Mitch crushed his mouth to hers, swallowing her oath. Her hands, which had been balled into fists at her side, rose to press against the unyielding line of his chest in a faint, impotent protest that shamed her.

It was an insult. An outrage. It was, Tory considered as his demanding lips savaged hers, wonderful. The passion that had been simmering between them did not build slowly, but exploded in a fireball of blinding heat, reaching out with tongues of flame and engulfing her. At first she struggled against him, but the friction of her breasts against his chest, of her thighs rubbing against his, only caused the flames to burn hotter. Faster.

The more he took, the more Tory demanded. There had never been any middle ground where this woman was concerned, Mitch remembered. Their relationship had always been like crossing a mine field: continual danger punctuated by blinding explosions. Primitive urges battered him inside, making his chest ache. His flesh burned, heat suffused him. He was trapped in a dark world of smoke and flame.

Just when Mitch was prepared to drag her to the floor and take her here, now, Tory pulled away.

She couldn't breathe. Ashamed at her response, yet unable to drag her eyes from his, she took a deep gulp of air. Then another. A third. As she tried to drag the lifesaving oxygen into her lungs, she realized that the last time she'd felt like this had been when she was nine years old. She'd been walking along the top rail of the fence in the north pasture of her grandfather's farm, pretending to be a high-wire circus performer, when she'd fallen. For what had seemed like hours she'd writhed on the ground, certain that her ribs must have punctured her heart and afraid she was going to die out there all alone.

Of course she hadn't died. Later her grandfather had explained that she'd simply knocked the wind out of her lungs. Now, as she struggled to regain her equilibrium, Tory wished that what was happening to her this time had such a simple explanation.

"Well, Cantrell, now that you've had your fun, it's time for you to leave so that I can repair my makeup before my next set."

Her voice was frail and shaky, proving despite her clipped words that she'd been no less affected by the kiss than he had been. Waiting until he was assured that his own voice would remain steady, Mitch thrust his hands into the pockets of his jeans.

"You can't ignore what just happened, Tory."

"Nothing happened."

His only response was a mockingly arched brow and an unwavering look. Tory had seen far stronger individuals than herself crumble before that steady gaze.

"All right," she admitted in frustration. "Perhaps things did get a little out of control. But it doesn't mean anything."

Mitch didn't blink.

"Dammit, all it means is that it's been a long time since I've been with a man," Tory insisted. "I'm only human, after all."

Mitch smiled at that. "Flesh and blood, so to speak."

The insinuation was there, just waiting for Tory to pick up on it. She refused. "So to speak. What just happened was simply a result of repressed sexual desire. Nothing more." In fact, it was like it had always been with Mitch—a case of spontaneous combustion. But remembering how spontaneous combustion had a way of blowing up in your face, she kept that little news bulletin to herself.

"You were always so good for my ego," Mitch murmured.

"And you always had sex on the brain," Tory countered.

Her skin gleamed like marble. But Mitch knew that it was a great deal warmer. And infinitely softer. Unable to resist, he reached out and brushed his fingers over the crest of her breasts. "I don't recall you complaining."

His slow, stroking touch was rekindling fires safer left banked. Tory snatched his hand away, turned back to the dressing table and began dragging her brush through the tousled hair of her wig. "That was then. This is now." The brush caught. "Damn," she muttered, tugging ineffectually.

"Here. Let me." Taking the brush from her hand, Mitch untangled the blond strands, then began moving the brush slowly down the long waves, smoothing them with the palm of one hand while he held the wig in place with the other. "I'm still having trouble getting used to you as a blonde."

His touch was strong, sure, yet gentle at the same time. Tory told herself that she shouldn't be enjoying it so much. But heaven help her, she was. "I'm not used to it myself. In fact, sometimes I catch a glimpse of myself in the mirror and wonder who that strange woman is."

"It's certainly glamorous." Mitch could feel her beginning to relax. "Although I have to admit that I prefer you as a brunette."

"Really? But my own hair is so boring." Compared to Amy's glowing blond locks, Tory had always felt that her own reddish-brown hair made her resemble a drab little wren.

"I like it. There was one morning, when you were still asleep, that I woke up with it spread across my chest. I remember playing with the strands in the sunlight and thinking that they looked like autumn leaves."

Tory reminded herself that Mitch was a man who made his living with words. Obviously words of seduction came easily for him. "Nice line," she allowed. "I imagine that it usually works wonders. With most women."

Mitch struggled to hold his rising temper. Once again he was struck by dual urges to shake her senseless or drag her to the floor and make love to her until they were both too exhausted and satiated to move. He suspected either—or both—would be eminently satisfying.

"But you're not most women, are you, Victoria?" His dark voice was filled with sensual innuendo.

Their gazes clashed in the mirror. "Please don't do this."

"Don't do what?" he asked gruffly. "Don't touch you?" He shaped her bare shoulders with his palms and was rewarded by the slight tremor she tried to hide. "Don't kiss you?" He lowered his head and pressed his mouth against the side of her neck. "Don't remember how you feel like liquid silk in my arms?"

"Mitch . . ." His low, hypnotic tone was making her weak at the knees. Tory was grateful she was sitting down; she wasn't certain she was capable of standing without support.

"The problem is, I do remember, Tory." He nuzzled her neck; her pulse jumped in response. "I remember everything. Your scent. How you taste." He rubbed a finger over her softly parted lips, then touched it to his own. "Those breathless little cries you make when I enter you." The fire was back, smoldering just beneath her skin. Tory closed her eyes as his hands cupped her breasts. "The way your soft brown eyes would widen when I took you over the edge."

His deep velvet voice, his stroking hands, the warmth of his breath against her neck were a lure and a challenge. *Yes. No. Touch me. Don't touch me.* Her mind and body were engaged in a war as old as time. Just when Tory was afraid that she'd succumb to his seductive touch, there was a sharp rapping on her dressing-room door.

"*Dos minutos, La Rubia,*" the stage manager announced. The abrupt intrusion affected Tory like a shock of icy water.

"*¡Gracias!*" she called out. Her blood pounded; she realized exactly how close she'd come to allowing her emotions to steamroller over her common sense. Just a few minutes alone with Mitchell Cantrell and she was not only ready to throw herself into his arms, she was on the verge of letting him ruin all her plans.

Shaking off his touch, she jumped from the stool and ran for the door. Before she could reach for the knob, she was abruptly whirled around. "Let go of me!"

"You're not going to spend the night with the general, Tory," Mitch told her.

"You can't stop me," she replied evenly, holding herself as rigid as a bar of cold steel.

Instead of appearing angry, Mitch suddenly seemed more amused than anything by her show of bravado. "Want to bet? Fifty dollars says that you end up spending the night with me instead."

"Your ego is not to be believed." Wondering how she'd even considered making love to such an arrogant, overbearing man, Tory glared at him.

"Fifty bucks," Mitch repeated.

"You're on," Tory declared.

"Terrific." Swinging her back against him, Mitch kissed her breathless yet again, then released her and left the dressing room. The self-satisfied, arrogant sound of his whistling echoed down the corridor.

As she made her way to the stage for her eleven o'clock show, Tory couldn't make up her mind whom she was more furious with: Mitch for initiating that deep, claiming kiss, or herself for enjoying it.

4

TORY HAD JUST BEGUN the final song of her set when a pair of uniformed soldiers entered the room, marched directly to the general's table and spoke to him in a low but audible buzz. The general pushed back his chair and strode off, the men at his heels.

After performing two brief encores, Tory returned to her dressing room to prepare for supper at the general's city home. Although she was loath to admit her fear, even to herself, her blood had turned to ice by the time she'd packed away her cosmetics.

She was just debating whether she dared dine alone with such a man when the stage manager arrived with a note from the general expressing his regrets, but explaining that a military emergency in the central valley necessitated his leaving the city.

He hoped to settle his business in three or four days' time, the note informed her, and until then he would cherish the memory of her dazzling beauty and lovely voice and look forward to escorting her to the American embassy's reception for La Rubia when he returned to Playa de Palma.

Impatient though she was to reveal the general's treachery, Tory felt like a condemned prisoner who'd just received a last-minute reprieve. She hated to admit it, but her encounter with General Ramirez, followed by that unsettling, passionate kiss she'd shared with Mitch, had left her feeling uncharacteristically unnerved.

All she needed was a good night's sleep, she assured herself. Then she'd be as good as new. Ready to reenter the fray.

IT WAS ABOUT TIME, Mitch reflected as he heard the mechanical sound of the elevator approaching the floor. Although he'd gotten rid of the general, it had crossed his mind as he sat in the dark, waiting for Tory to return to her suite, that she could have gotten accosted by some other would-be suitor.

Single, attractive women were always at some peril alone at night in Playa de Palma, but dressed as she was in that skintight red dress that displayed more gleaming flesh than it covered, Tory was definitely at risk. He had just decided to go look for her when he heard the elevator. Relieved, Mitch's heartbeat returned to normal.

Tory gasped when she turned on the light and saw the man sprawled on the couch. Recognition dawned; fear turned to irritation. "What are you doing here?"

"Waiting for you."

"Gee, I'm so sorry I wasn't back in time to offer you a drink," she said, looking pointedly at the snifter of brandy he was holding between his palms.

"That's all right." Mitch flashed her his world-famous grin. Tory had no doubt that during his years as a foreign correspondent, that dazzling, boyish smile had undoubtedly charmed women from Tulsa to Timbuktu. "I helped myself."

"So I see."

He nodded toward the second glass sitting on the marble coffee table. "I poured one for you, too."

"What made you think I'd even be back here tonight?" she challenged. "In case you've forgotten, I'm supposed to be having a late supper with the general."

"I haven't forgotten a thing, Victoria," he said quietly. "But since the general was unexpectedly called out of town, I thought you might be willing to settle for my company instead."

Tory studied him through narrowed eyes. "What did you do?"

"What makes you think I did anything?"

"I suppose it's a coincidence that a sudden military emergency occurs on the very night I'm supposed to be dining alone with General Ramirez?"

"There's always trouble with rebels in the central valley. Why should tonight be any different?"

"I didn't say anything about the central valley."

"Didn't you?" Mitch asked guilelessly.

"No." Tory put her hands up on her hips, conveniently forgetting that only minutes ago she had been relieved when the general was unable to keep their engagement. "And there's no point in lying, because this little operation has your fingerprints all over it, Mitch Cantrell!"

"You're just angry because I'm going to win the bet."

"The damn bet doesn't have anything to do with it. I'm furious because you're about to ruin all my plans." The heavy wig had her head in a vise. She yanked off the blond disguise with a sigh of relief, allowing her own dark hair to tumble over her shoulders.

"You don't have to yell, Tory." Slowly, deliberately, he unfolded his tall body from the couch and walked over to her. He touched her. Just a hand to her hair. Nothing more. But it was enough to cause excitement to ripple up her spine. "If you really want to keep me from messing things up, there's a simple enough solution."

Her lips were so dry. Tory resisted the urge to lick them. "Nothing's ever simple about you," she managed as his fingers played with her hair. "In fact, you're the most complex man I've ever met."

"Really?" Mitch murmured. "But I've been accused of being immeasurably simple."

"I find that difficult to believe." Tory struggled to ignore the warmth created by his hand at the back of her neck.

"It's true. Alanna accused me of having a Peter Pan complex."

"I've been told the same thing," she admitted with a reluctant smile.

"Oh?" He bent his head, fascinated by her scent. It was at the same time sultry and innocent, sweet and seductive. It was, Mitch judged, a great deal like the lady herself. "Was it perchance any particular individual who accused you of such a dastardly personality flaw?"

His breath was warm against her neck, she could feel the warmth emanating from his body. She wanted him, Tory admitted. Desperately. But the past had taught her that want—need—was not enough. "It was a man."

"A special man?"

"I thought so at the time." Shaking herself free of Mitch's light touch, Tory crossed the room, picked up the brandy snifter and sat down in the corner of the sofa. "Brian was a British economist. We met at a European economic summit in Geneva."

"And he swept you off your feet?" Mitch asked as he joined her. He hadn't forgotten what she'd said about all women wanting to be swept off their feet at one time or another.

Seeming to relax for the first time since her arrival in La Paz, Tory chuckled softly. The warm, bubbly sound entered his blood with the effervescence of champagne.

"Hardly. My plane had been delayed in New York because of fog. By the time I arrived in Geneva I was already late for the opening session, so I just grabbed my bags and ran for a cab."

"I think I see this one coming."

"It *was* rather clichéd," Tory allowed. "You can imagine how I felt when I started to unpack and discovered three gray flannel suits and a tuxedo from Savile Row."

"I would have loved to see the guy's face when he found all that silk and satin I put away this afternoon."

She laughed again. Mitch took a long drink of brandy. "Brian said that after opening my suitcase, he knew he had to locate its owner."

Mitch hated the guy without having ever met him. It was enough to know that he'd touched Tory. Kissed her. Loved with her, and even worse, laughed with her. "So what happened?"

Surprised by his black tone, Tory glanced at him, experiencing a surge of pure feminine pleasure when she viewed the naked jealousy in his eyes. "The romance was doomed from the start. I just didn't want to see it. Brian wanted someone to help him carry on the family name along with all its lofty British traditions, a woman who'd willingly put her own drives aside to give birth to a dynasty, so that the noble line of Montgomery would not die out."

"Sounds like a lot of responsibility," Mitch observed. And certainly not Tory Martin's cup of tea.

"I thought I could manage it in the beginning," Tory explained, not wanting to reveal that at the time she'd been desperate for a stable home for her troubled sister. Tory had thought that if she could make her sister a member of a real family, one with strong, enduring, century-old roots, Amy might actually settle down.

"So what happened?"

"We were getting dressed for Ascot when I got a call from the London bureau chief that there had been a terrorist bombing near the prime minister's home. Naturally I had to tell Brian that I couldn't attend the races with him."

Mitch nodded. He would have done the very same thing. "Naturally."

"Unfortunately, Brian couldn't understand why some other reporter couldn't cover the bombing."

"What you mean is that he couldn't understand why you'd want to," Mitch corrected knowingly.

"That, too," Tory agreed on a sigh. "We had a terrible argument."

Again Mitch wasn't surprised. When she was in top form, Tory could probably cause Mother Teresa to lose her cool. "People fight," he said. "Even lovers." He ran his hand down her hair. "Especially lovers."

Tory knew that if she lived to be a hundred years old, she'd never forget the distaste that had been stamped on

Brian's aristocratic features. "A Montgomery never argues."

"You're kidding."

"No," she insisted. "Not ever. In fact, I doubt if the walls of that old manor house have heard a single raised voice in five hundred years. Until mine, that is." She sighed again. "All those ancestors whose sober portraits line the entry hall are undoubtedly still reeling in their graves."

Mitch considered that for a moment, recalling that one of the most satisfying things about fighting with Tory had always been the making up afterwards. "Obviously they've diluted the noble old Montgomery line so badly that they needed to bring in some feisty American blood."

Tory laughed, as she was supposed to. "You're incorrigible."

"Guilty. But so are you," he pointed out. "I hope Montgomery didn't break your heart."

"No." Tory grew reflective. "To tell you the truth, I was relieved when he asked for his grandmother's ring back."

"His loss."

It would have been impossible to miss the desire in his husky voice. Although she had never considered herself a coward, Tory didn't dare look at him. She wouldn't. She couldn't. Heaven help her, she did.

Mitch saw the questions swirling in her eyes. Questions he wished he knew the answers to himself. The only thing he did know was that the way she was looking at him reminded him of the first time he'd kissed her.

"That first night," he murmured, lifting their joined hands to his lips. "You were afraid."

Tory found herself wondering how Alanna Cantrell could have possibly sent this man away. Yet hadn't Tory herself sent Mitch off to Beirut with nothing more than a breezy goodbye? She'd also spent eight years regretting her action.

"Not of the rockets," she managed, through lips that had suddenly turned to stone.

"No. You were never afraid of the guns," he remembered. "In fact you were so unrepentantly fearless, I was terrified that you'd get killed chasing after some damn exclusive."

They'd fought over what he considered her fool-hardy behavior on more than one occasion. Each time Tory had not hesitated to point out that Mitch had never been one to turn his back on a fast-breaking story. No matter how dangerous.

"Dammit, that's different!" he'd shouted. "You're a woman!"

"I'm a reporter!" she'd screamed back, then stormed out of the room, slamming the door behind her. And much as she'd wanted to remain angry with him, before long she'd returned and they'd spent hours making love. If nothing had been resolved, neither had wanted to rock the highly unstable boat by mentioning it.

"I was afraid of you," she admitted now.

His brows drew together. "Of me? Why?"

"I was never quite sure," she said. "Actually, if you want the unvarnished truth, I was probably more afraid of myself." She drew in a deep, shuddering breath. "Of me loving you."

Reaching up, she traced the familiar planes of his face with her fingertips, frowning when she discovered that his cheekbone had been broken. The difference in his appearance was imperceptible, but she could feel the dip in the bone under her stroking touch. To feel the proof of his torture was more painful than she could have imagined. Her eyes filled with hot tears.

Mitch had witnessed Tory dodging enemy bullets. He'd seen her slog through the jungle mud, fighting off mosquitoes the size of B-52 bombers. He'd seen her interview displaced peasants and heads of state with the same unwavering concentration. He'd watched her eyes widen with surprise and pleasure when she'd experienced her first orgasm. But never had he seen Victoria Martin cry. Now he watched the silver ribbon of tears stream silently down her face and was immeasurably moved.

"Tory." He brushed the moisture away with his knuckles. "Sweetheart, what's the matter?"

"I hate them," she said in a furious burst of passion that he found far more familiar than her earlier grief. "I hate them for hurting you."

"Don't." His hand moved from her cheek to the back of her neck, holding her gaze to his. "It's over," he said softly.

Was it? Tory wondered. As she looked into his eyes, trying not to see the thin white scar cutting its way across his right lid, she wondered if anything was really ever over.

"I don't understand," she whispered.

Mitch managed a wry smile. "That makes two of us."

If she didn't stop looking at him that way, he was going to rise to the sensual invitation in her soft brown eyes and take her to bed. He'd been celibate for six long years—five of them courtesy of his holy-war captors, the past twelve months by choice. It was obvious, Mitch concluded, that such an unnatural state would be bound to take its toll sooner or later.

He slanted her a speculative look. "I think perhaps this is where you tell me what you're doing here, Tory. The truth, this time," he demanded quietly.

She was growing as tired of Mitch asking that question as he clearly was of asking it. Breathing a sigh of frustration, Tory realized that the time had come to face the music.

"It's about my sister."

"Amy."

Once again Tory envied Mitch his total recall. "Amy," she repeated softly, looking down at her hands as she felt that now-familiar pain deep in her heart. "She's in a hospital in Miami. The doctors say she'll be all right eventually, but it isn't going to be easy. And Amy never has been very strong. At least not emotionally."

Tory didn't add that this latest incident had caused her to face the unpalatable fact that her own continual big-sister-to-the-rescue behavior might have contributed to Amy's inner weakness.

Saying nothing, Mitch drew her into his arms. At first she stiffened, but when he began to gently stroke her hair, she rested her head upon his shoulder and closed her eyes. Slowly the words began to come.

"From the time we were little girls, I tried to do the right thing for Amy." The tears threatened again. Tory pressed the heels of her hands against her closed eyes. "I knew the kind of men she always fell in love with. I knew how they hurt her. But I never thought that any of them would try to kill her."

His hand stopped in midstroke. "Someone tried to kill your sister?"

Tory rose and walked across the room to the window. The moon was a gleaming silver dollar hanging high in the sky, turning the waters of the Caribbean to a dazzling argent. Amy had looked out at the same ocean, had probably walked along that glistening white sand. Perhaps she'd even stopped to pick up a pink seashell that the tides had washed up onto the shore.

Knowing that the best way to encourage someone to talk was to keep quiet, Mitch didn't say anything. He simply waited.

Tory wrapped her arms around herself and took a deep breath. "I tried to make arrangements to come to Playa de Palma and stop her before she got herself into serious trouble, but then I got word that she was in the hospital."

"She was here? In La Paz?"

"Actually she was working at this hotel."

Mitch recalled a photo Tory had shown him of her sister. She'd been wearing a brief pair of shorts and a halter top and laughing into the camera. And although she'd only been in her early teens at the time, it had been easy to see that she was going to be a knockout.

"I assume that she didn't come all the way to La Paz to work in the hotel as a maid," he said.

Tory spun around. Her eyes flashed a dangerous warning. "No. And it's not what you're implying, either."

He held up his hand. "I wasn't implying anything, Tory."

"Yes, you were." Two red flags waved in her cheeks. "Amy was not working as a prostitute."

"All right. So what was she?"

"A singer." Tory glared at him, defying him to call her a liar.

"That's what you're doing here, isn't it?" he said wonderingly. "That's also why you've changed your appearance. So you can smoke out whoever tried to kill your little sister."

"I already have."

Damn. He'd been afraid of that. "I don't think I want to hear this, Tory."

"General Ramirez tried to kill Amy," she said. "Or at least paid someone to do it."

The muscles in Mitch's stomach tightened. "So you've come all the way to Playa de Palma, pretending to be a cabaret singer, to get revenge on the general."

"Exactly."

Mitch swore. Eight years. Eight long years and the woman hadn't changed one iota. She was still every bit as headstrong and foolish as she'd been when they'd first met. "You're crazy." He covered the distance between them in two long strides.

Tory tilted her chin. Instead of grief, fury now flashed in her eyes. "It really was the general," she insisted, telling him about Amy's letter, about the blackmail scheme. About her sister's misbegotten hopes of marriage. "So you see I really do have proof."

"Damn your proof." He grabbed hold of her shoulders so hard that he almost threw her off balance. "Don't you realize this is his country? Ramirez makes the rules here, Victoria. He's the marshal, the judge, the jury and the executioner. And if you think I'm going to just sit by and watch you get that lovely head chopped off—"

"That isn't going to happen." The anger was still there, but now it was iced over.

Mitch tried a different tack. "Look," he said, lowering his voice, "why don't you just let me see the letter?"

"Are you saying you'll help me?"

"No. I'm saying that if Ramirez really did attempt to kill your sister, for whatever reason, I'll do what I can to make certain that he pays for his crime. But you're going back to the States. Or Lithuania. Or wherever the hell you were when you came up with this lunatic idea."

"It's not a lunatic idea."

"Any idea that has you dressing up like your sister and coming on to a homicidal, probably paranoid egomaniac is a damn lunatic idea," he shot back.

"Amy was on to something," Tory insisted. "All I have to do is get into the general's house and find out what it was."

She was really something. Mitch wondered how he was going to stop Tory, short of tying her up in a strait-jacket. He didn't understand hate. Even after his years of captivity, he'd found that he couldn't hate his captors the way people expected. The situation had been too complex to separate everyone into black hats and white. Some of the people who'd held him hostage had been evil monsters, others had seemed to be men who under normal conditions could have been thoughtful, decent individuals.

Unfortunately there hadn't been anything normal about the holy war going on in Lebanon. And Mitch had witnessed hatred often enough during those years in the Middle East to recognize that most volatile of emotions in Tory. She hated the general with a white-hot passion. And she would stop at nothing to achieve her revenge.

"So why don't you just ask Amy what she knows?"

"I tried. She has amnesia."

"You realize that this is sounding more and more like some television soap opera?" Mitch observed dryly.

"Don't you think I know that?" Tory stormed on. "But Amy insists that she doesn't remember a thing prior to the accident, and the doctors say that amnesia is a natural occurrence after a concussion."

"So why didn't you wait for her memory to return?"

"Because the doctors also said it might not, and . . ." Her voice faded as she realized she was about to reveal a deep-seated suspicion she hadn't wanted to face.

"And?" he coaxed softly. Insistently.

"And there's an outside chance she may be lying," Tory admitted reluctantly.

"Because she was involved in the general's so-called illegal activities?"

"No." She'd already considered that possibility and discarded it. "Look, I'll admit Amy is spoiled. She is also immature and high-strung. But my sister is not a criminal."

"Yet she was willing to marry one," Mitch pointed out.

"That was just a fantasy," Tory declared in a voice that was not as strong as she would have liked. "She would have come to her senses sooner or later."

"I'll bet." He crossed his arms over his chest. "I suppose that you plan to waltz right into Ramirez's house, open the safe behind the van Gogh, riffle through his private papers and uncover the smoking gun?"

"There's a safe behind a van Gogh?"

"Isn't there always? In the movies?"

Her hope vanished. "Oh. You shouldn't tease me, Mitch. Because this isn't a movie."

"Now that's the first intelligent point you've made since you hit town, sweetheart," he growled.

She recognized the voice as the one he'd used the time she'd made the mistake of taking a photograph of a military policeman beating up a civilian protesting martial law. When the policeman had insisted that she hand over her camera, she'd steadfastly refused, a behavior which had resulted in her being arrested. When Mitch had shown up at the jail to bail her out, she'd been relieved. Thirty minutes later, when he was still yelling at her, Tory had begun to wish she'd taken her chances with the jailer.

When Tory met his challenging glare with a level, defiant look of her own, Mitch muttered an oath. "You're not going to back away from this, are you?"

"No."

"What if I tell you that I'm not about to let you get yourself mixed up in anything so dangerous?"

His eyes were gleaming with a rigid determination she'd seen before. Tory held her ground. "I don't recall asking your permission."

"So what proof do you really have? And what's the damn plan?"

His tone wasn't the least bit encouraging, but Tory saw the reluctant interest in his eyes and realized that although she'd always preferred to work alone, this might just be one instance where having a partner would not be such a bad idea. Especially one who possessed Mitch's obvious survival skills. It took her exactly three seconds to make up her mind.

"I'll get Amy's letter."

She left the room, and a moment later Mitch heard her rummaging around in her makeup kit. Dragging a hand over his face, he wondered what kind of trouble the woman was getting them into this time.

5

MITCH READ THE LETTER through once. Twice. Three times. Finally, just when Tory thought that her nerves were going to snap, he refolded the thin airmail paper and put it down on the coffee table with a long, weary sigh.

She watched, waiting impatiently for him to say something. Anything. Instead he rose from the sofa and stood by the window, staring out at the moonlit sea while he sipped his brandy. A tense silence settled over the room.

"It must be something in the genes," he told her at last.

"What?"

He turned toward her, pinning her with an intense stare. "This penchant you Martin women have for getting into trouble."

Her cheeks flamed. "You can't possibly compare what Amy was doing to—"

He cut her off with a vicious slice of his hand. "That's precisely what I'm doing," he said, almost grinding out the words. "Oh, I'm not accusing you of planning to cold-bloodedly sleep with the guy. The way I figure it, you're actually naive enough to believe that you can just flutter those thick lashes like Scarlett O'Hara and keep Ramirez interested enough to let you get close to him, but not so close that you'll have to go to bed with him."

"I have no intention of going to bed with him!" she shouted.

"So, since we're agreed that you're not going to let the general score," Mitch continued scathingly, "exactly how far did you decide to let the creep go to keep him hooked?"

"I thought I'd play it by ear."

Mitch nodded with grim satisfaction; he'd suspected as much. She'd definitely been watching too many spy movies. "It probably wouldn't be a bad idea to set limits, at least in your own mind," he suggested. "After all, you did let the guy put his slimy hands on you in the dressing room."

The memory of Ramirez's fingers on her shoulders sent a chill up Tory's spine. "I didn't have any choice."

"You always have a choice, Tory," he said gravely. "Right now I can think of several."

She just bet he could. "I'm not going back," she declared mutinously.

"Fine. So, since we've eliminated the only sensible one, I suppose we'd better try out a few others. Such as the one where you lure him into confessing his darkest secrets. Including the attempted murder of your sister."

"I certainly hadn't expected him to confess."

"Then you must be going to drug his champagne during that intimate dinner for two. Thus giving you an opportunity to search his house while he's passed out."

Tory didn't answer, but her guilty expression gave her away.

"Damn. I was afraid of that," Mitch said with yet another sigh. "Tell me, Mata Hari, what are you going to do if the general pounces before you have a chance to spike his drink?"

"I'm not completely inexperienced, Mitch," she insisted. "What makes you think I can't handle a little flirtation?"

"A little flirtation, she calls it," he muttered. "Don't you realize that this is a man used to getting everything he wants? When he wants it?"

Dragging his hand through his hair, Mitch inhaled deeply, a fierce frustration fighting to take over what little patience he had left. Ruthless with himself, he held his temper under control. "When you do get around to setting limits, what do you intend to do if the general chooses to ignore them? What if his hands decide to rove somewhere other than your lovely shoulders?"

When his knowing blue eyes drifted to the curve of her breasts, more revealed than concealed by the clinging red dress, Tory paled. She snatched up an emerald satin throw pillow from the corner of the sofa and clutched it against her chest. "I'll simply insist that he stop."

"I see." Mitch rubbed his chin thoughtfully, as if imagining the scenario. "So exactly how far are you willing to go to lure the guy into submission?"

"You make it sound so tacky," she complained.

"And you make it sound like something from an Ian Fleming plot." His anger was getting harder and harder to restrain. What was worse, he suspected the woman knew it. There had been times in the past when he'd suspected that she'd enjoyed making him lose control. "Dammit, Tory, as reckless as you always were, you never stooped to a stupid, idiotic, dangerous stunt like this to get a story."

The color returned to her cheeks. Redder, hotter. "Perhaps that's because this a lot more important than any story!" Now it was her turn to flare. "She is my sister, Mitch. And Ramirez nearly killed her. I know he did."

His eyes softened with genuine compassion. She saw the anger fade from those intense depths, giving way to concern as he crossed the room and gathered her into his arms. "I know. That's why we're going to have to think out our strategy very, very carefully."

His arms were strong, capable of offering protection as well as comfort. For a brief, wonderful moment, Tory rested her head on Mitch's shoulder and allowed herself to bask in the soothing touch of his powerful hands as they stroked her back.

"*Our?*" As his words belatedly sank in, Tory tilted her head back and looked at him. "You're going to help me?"

Do I have a choice? Mitch could have asked in return as he breathed in the soft scent lingering in her hair, but didn't. He felt frustrated and stymied, and every instinct he possessed told him that if he agreed to go along with Tory's cockamamy plan, he was just as crazy as she was.

"Someone has to," he said.

"But you still don't approve."

"No. I can't honestly say that I do." How could he possibly condone anything that could end up getting her killed? He couldn't. That was why he was going to have to make certain she remained safe. Until he could convince her to give up what had to be an impossible quest.

"Then why?"

His fingers brushed her skin as he touched the side of her face. "Let's just consider it my good deed for the day."

His touch was light, unthreatening, but strangely possessive. Unwilling to let him know that she was so susceptible to him, Tory let out her breath. Slowly. Carefully.

"Thank you."

Her grave tone was at odds with the unwilling desire in her eyes. Mitch found them both irresistible. "You're welcome." He'd done his duty. And now, to satisfy himself, he bent his head and lowered his mouth to hers.

It was only a softest whisper of a kiss. Unthreatening. Undemanding. Infinitely gentle. When he nibbled his way from one corner of her mouth to the other, she sighed; when his teeth tugged lightly at her lower lip, she felt the response deep inside her. It was a slow, insistent tug. A warmth that began somewhere in her lower regions and spread thickly outward.

His tongue tempted; Tory surrendered. With a soft moan she wrapped her arms around him and allowed her mind to empty.

As he tasted, for the first time in too many years, the sweet, warm flavor of a woman, Mitch remembered in vivid, sensual detail how it had been to make love to Tory. Those erotic memories alone were enough to arouse him.

"Tory." Her name was a hot breeze against her lips as he feasted upon her mouth. Lost somewhere between yesterday and the present, Mitch pressed her against him, one strong hand firmly against her hip, the other tangled possessively in her hair. As he deepened the kiss, degree by glorious degree, the past rose up to mingle seductively with the present.

It was happening all over again. The rigid lines of his body took her breath away. His clever mouth bemused her; his wicked hands bewitched her. Nothing had changed. Time shifted, like the colorful fragments in a kaleidoscope, and she was again young, foolish and madly in love with the only man who'd ever possessed the power to break her heart.

His lips blazed a trail of sparks up the side of her face. "Come to bed with me, Tory," he murmured against her ear.

She wanted to. Dear Lord, how she'd love to recapture their seductive past, if only for this one magical night. But she had not come all the way to La Paz to make love to Mitch Cantrell—as delicious a prospect as that admittedly was. She'd come here for revenge. Her task was dangerous; it was going to take every single ounce of her concentration, and if she allowed herself to be continually distracted this way, she was certain to fail.

Shaken, Tory dropped her arms to her sides and drew away. "Good try. But it's not going to work, Cantrell." Her voice was thin and trembled badly.

Mitch stared at her, his expression as fierce as she'd ever seen it. And that was saying something, Tory reflected. Stories of Mitch Cantrell's temper were legion, some exaggerated, most not.

"What the hell are you talking about now?"

"I was referring to your clever ruse to seduce me into giving up my plan."

He brought his hand under her chin and held it there. "Is that what you think I was doing?"

Tory's wide eyes were dark and unsure. "Wasn't it?"

"At the moment it was the farthest thing from my mind."

"But you wanted me to go to bed with you."

"Of course I did. But not because of any power game."

"Then why?"

"I'd say that should be obvious, Victoria." Without taking his eyes from hers, Mitch ran his free hand up her side. When his long fingers skimmed her breast, he was rewarded by her sharp intake of breath. "I want you."

It was not, Tory admitted reluctantly what she'd secretly wanted to hear. Still, even as she felt the sting, she accepted it. She and Mitch had been together for three months—ninety-one tumultuous, passionate days—and he'd never once told her he loved her. Why should this time be any different?

But it was, Tory realized. Because this time she was different.

"And I want you. I'm not going to lie and say that I don't." She pressed her hand against his cheek, almost weakening as she felt the short stubble against her palm and remembered the way his unshaven beard had felt against her breasts. "But sometimes wanting isn't enough."

Nothing about Tory Martin had ever been easy, Mitch reminded himself. But backing away now, when he wanted to carry her into the adjoining bedroom, where he would slowly undress her, tasting each little bit of freed flesh . . .

"Isn't it? We'll see," he murmured, fighting down the renewed surge of desire stimulated by his fantasy.

"Mitch," she said warningly.

"If you don't trust me, Victoria, perhaps you'd better find yourself another accomplice." His voice was very smooth and very quiet. And, Tory estimated, very dangerous.

"No." She shook her head. "You're right," she said in a soft little tone of surrender that he suspected was feigned. He'd never known Tory to give up so easily. "I need help to get Ramirez. And there isn't anyone better qualified than you."

"You're right about that, sweetheart." He kissed her again, pleased with the soft, feminine tremor of her lips beneath his. Before she could protest, he released her. "You'd better get some sleep. We've got a lot of work to do tomorrow."

Nervous though she was about being in such close proximity to a man who could make her head swim just by looking at her, Tory knew that if anyone could uncover the general's treacherous secret, it was Mitch. His worldwide network of informants was envied by both print and television correspondents alike. Not to mention certain members of various covert government agencies.

"I am tired." A deep, bone-wearying exhaustion began to steamroller over her earlier desire.

"You've had a long day."

"Yes." When Mitch didn't appear to be in any hurry to leave, she glanced pointedly at the door. "I really do appreciate your offer to help. What time can I expect you tomorrow?"

"I'm not leaving."

She was too tired to deal with another seduction attempt. "Really, Mitch . . ."

"Tory, Tory," he murmured, "you are going to have to learn to trust me. As much as I want to make love to you, sweetheart, I'm not the kind of man to take advantage of an obviously exhausted woman. Besides, I'm not sure my ego could take you falling asleep on me just when we got to the good part."

"But . . ."

He curved his fingers around her shoulders and turned her in the direction of the bedroom. "Go to bed, Tory. I'll just sack out here on the couch in case the general discovers that his so-called emergency was merely business as usual and decides to pay you a middle-of-the-night visit."

He had a point, she thought sleepily. While Mitch was not the kind of man to force himself upon a sleeping woman, she knew that General Ramirez would not possess the same moral standards.

Her mind numbed by exhaustion, she washed her face, brushed her teeth, undressed and climbed into bed. The minute her head hit the pillow, she fell into a deep, dreamless sleep.

THE SMELL OF COFFEE woke her. That and the soft cooing of a pigeon perched outside her window. Tory stared around the room, her sleep-hazed mind refusing to recognize her strange surroundings. Then she remembered. She was in La Paz. With Mitch.

Just his name was enough to warm her to the core. She shouldn't feel this way, Tory told herself. She shouldn't let herself feel this way. Mitch was still a gypsy. As was she. As soon as she accomplished her revenge, they'd both go their separate ways. As they'd done in the past.

Tory loved her work. She thrived on the challenge, the fast pace, never knowing from one day to the next where in the world she'd be living, what fast-breaking story she'd be covering. She was one of the lucky ones, she reminded herself as she threw back the covers and went into the bathroom. One of the few people on earth able to do exactly what she wanted with her life.

So why, she asked herself, turning her face up to the pelting warm spray of the shower, did she suddenly feel as if something was missing?

After she'd showered and dressed, Tory found Mitch on the balcony, studying a sheaf of papers. On the table was an insulated carafe of coffee, a bowl of tropical fruit and a basket of freshly baked pastries.

"I'm sorry I slept so late," she greeted him.

"You had a long, stressful day," he said, looking up from the papers. He poured her a cup of the fragrant coffee. "That, along with jet lag, would make anyone sleep in."

She sat down at the table across from Mitch and eyed him judiciously, trying to find some flaw that would make him look less attractive. His face was deeply tanned, the lines extending outward from his eyes adding character rather than age. His hair in the late-morning light gleamed silver and gold.

"You need a haircut."

Mitch grinned. "Now you sound like my boss. He's always telling me I look like a hippie, which forces me to remind him that as head of network news, he should know that hippies went out with bell-bottom jeans, love beads and peace signs."

"It's not all that long," Tory said, struck with a sudden urge to run her fingers through the waves brushing his collar. "But you'd never be able to get a job anchoring."

"Perhaps that's why I don't get a haircut as often as those other guys," he suggested. "Keeps me out of the running."

"I heard you were offered the anchor spot after you were freed last year."

"For once the rumors were true."

"You turned it down?" She knew more than one correspondent who'd sell his grandmother at a bargain-basement price for a chance at the network's top spot.

"You know me, Tory."

Yes, she did. Mitch was no more capable of settling down than she was. When that idea had her feeling strangely sad, she directed her gaze over the calm blue Caribbean and sipped her cinnamon-spiced coffee.

"I also heard you were writing a book about your experiences in Lebanon. That must have been difficult. Reliving everything."

"Actually," Mitch said, "it was kind of cathartic. I worked through a lot of conflicted feelings. . . . It'll be out in about six months."

"I'd like to read it."

"I'd like you to," he said simply.

They exchanged a look that lasted just a heartbeat too long. Flustered, Tory glanced at the papers in his hands. "What are those?"

"The general's bank records."

She stared at him. "How on earth—?"

"Now, Tory," Mitch reprimanded. "You know a good reporter never divulges his sources."

"But it's only ten o'clock in the morning," she protested. "The bank's only been open for half an hour."

"Long enough."

She shook her head with admiration. "You're amazing."

"Remind me to have you write a letter of recommendation to the network the next time my contract comes up for renewal." His smile faded. "You're right, by the way."

"About what?"

"The general is into something."

She knew it. Adrenaline surged through her veins, mingling with the caffeine to jolt her fully awake. "What?"

"There's a definite pattern to his deposits." He put a ledger sheet in front of her and ran his fingers down the columns. "As you can see, he's been making a pretty hefty cash deposit on the first and fifteenth of every month."

Tory's eye widened at the number of zeros filling the pale green columns. "No wonder he can live so well," she breathed. "Over a few months that must amount to millions and millions of dollars."

"He's sure as hell not a candidate for food stamps. Look at the withdrawal column."

Tory followed his finger. "He takes it back out the same day? Why? What's the point?"

"I think it's more a case of transferring all that cash to somewhere safe," Mitch said. "After all, he can't keep it hidden under his mattress."

"So he moves it to a Swiss account. Or a Bahamian one."

"More likely a Panamanian or Bahamian one," Mitch suggested. "It'd be closer. They are also still intensely secretive, while the Swiss have been becoming more cooperative about turning over criminal account numbers in recent years."

"Where do you think he gets all that cash?" Tory mused. "Do you suppose it's from the U.S.?"

"Skimming from U.S. aid dollars is starting to get tricky," Mitch answered. "Plus, government funds aren't given in actual cash." He rubbed his jaw. "From what I can see, except for the usual petty graft and nepotism, the general's pretty clean when it comes to U.S. aid expenditures. Clean enough, anyway, for government work."

"Then what else? Drugs?"

He shook his head. "I considered that possibility and discarded it."

Tory wasn't certain that she liked the way Mitch was suddenly taking over. This was her problem. Amy was her sister. And although she couldn't deny that she didn't welcome Mitch's help, she didn't appreciate him running the show.

"*You* considered the possibility?"

He nodded in acknowledgment. "And discarded it."

"So that's it?" she asked incredulously. "We just ignore the obvious?" She slammed her cup onto the saucer. Coffee spilled over the rim and onto the table. "I suppose we're to believe that the general is making all those big bucks selling his flowers to the States? What's he doing? Getting kickbacks on Rose Bowl floats?"

Moving the papers out of the way, Mitch took a napkin and wiped at the spreading brown stain. "We're not going to ignore anything, Tory," he said, appearing not to notice her scathing tone. "But don't forget, I just finished an in-depth report on drugs in Latin America."

"So I suppose that makes you the world's leading expert?" A mocking challenge glittered in her brown eyes.

"No. But I do know that the general's name didn't come up anywhere in my investigation." He refilled her cup. "It'd be nice if things were that cut-and-dried, because then we could call in the big governmental guns to help us out. But it's too easy a solution and I don't think it fits the guy's profile."

Frustrated, she pushed herself out of the chair and leaned against the balcony railing, looking over the palm-studded expanse of white sand toward the sea. The tall, fringed date palms were what gave the city its name. Pink flamingos strutted along the water's edge, while pelicans preened on the breakwater. A pair of wind surfers rode the gentle swell, skimming along the shimmering turquoise water like brightly colored dragonflies. On the horizon a fishing boat chugged slowly, trailing its wide nets behind it, followed by a flock of gulls.

Despite its violent political history, despite the uncivilized, ferociously dense interior rain forest and the volcanoes that erupted with destructive regularity, La Paz was a country of exquisite beauty. It was also, Tory reminded herself, a place of intrigue and murder.

"If not drugs," she said slowly, turning back to Mitch, "then what?"

"I have no idea." Mitch was quite truthful. He was afraid that if he told Tory about his current project, she'd take off on her own before he could get proof of the general's illegal activities. "But I'm working on it. In the meantime you may as well have some breakfast."

"I'm not hungry."

"Nonsense," he said dismissively. "You have to keep your strength up." Ignoring her muttered response, he spread some nutmeg jam onto a huge, flaky croissant, put it on a plate with a few slices of mango and papaya and pushed it toward her.

"I'd forgotten how bossy you are," she said, flinging herself back into her chair.

Something that could have been amusement or annoyance flickered in his eyes as he skimmed a glance over her. "And I'd forgotten how beautiful you are."

Her hair was back in its familiar thick braid, revealing her high, slanting cheekbones. Her skin was not as deeply tanned as when he'd seen her last. In those days, weeks of following the general's rebel troops had darkened it to a rich, dark mahogany. Today her complexion was a soft honey color that allowed the roses to show in her cheeks.

The vivid pink and orange halter dress left her shoulders, arms and back bare. Her legs were bare as well and suddenly he wanted to take her somewhere hushed and dark, where they could listen to the sound of the tropical rain on the roof and he could feel those long legs wrapped around him. Because the hours he'd spent waiting for her to wake had been too long and lonely, he reached out and took her hand in his.

"Mitch," she warned softly, feeling that dangerous, familiar warmth his touch aroused. "Please, don't." She took a deep breath. "I'm not going to try to deny that I'm attracted to you. But I'm sorry, I'm really not into casual sex."

"Good. Because there's nothing casual about the way you make me feel." Without taking his eyes from hers, he lifted her fingers to his lips. "I've been thinking about last night. About how right you felt in my arms."

"Last night never should have happened," she insisted in a voice she wished was stronger. "I never should have let it happen. I really am sorry, Mitch, but—"

"Amazing," he murmured.

Inside, Tory was a mass of tingling nerves and aching confusion. Outside, her expression remained one of studious control. "What's amazing?" With the last sliver of willpower she tugged her hand free.

"That you take so much responsibility onto those gorgeous shoulders. Your sister. Your job. Now last night." Lightly he traced her ear, toying with the pink seashell earring. "We shared some kisses, Victoria. You enjoyed them." His finger trailed down her neck, feeling like a sparkler against her sun-warmed skin. "I enjoyed them." Across her collarbone. "We enjoyed them together."·

With deliberate leisure, his treacherous finger glided over her breast. "I wanted you. You wanted me, but said no." If Mitch knew that his caress was making her weak, he pretended not to notice. "That was your privilege. You have nothing to apologize for, sweetheart."

It was so easy for him, Tory told herself. All he had to do was look at her. Touch her. And she'd fall right into his arms. Well, perhaps she'd been that foolish once. But not this time. She drew back, aroused and all too aware how helpless she appeared every time she was with him.

"I wasn't apologizing for saying no. I was merely suggesting that I should never have given you the wrong idea."

"It wasn't the wrong idea. But perhaps the timing was a little off," he conceded.

During these past hours, while he'd waited for his contact to arrive with the bank records, he'd thought back over everything that had happened between Tory and himself and decided he probably should have given her time to adjust to the idea that they were together again. After all, he'd known for weeks she was coming to La Paz; she hadn't been expecting him at all. On top of that, she'd been trying to pull off that idiotic confrontation with the general, all while suffering from jet lag.

He'd just have to take things more slowly. Mitch remembered a time when patience had been an unknown quality. In that regard, perhaps his enforced five-year stay in Lebanon had done him some good, after all.

"Are you laughing at me?" Tory asked, seeing a faint smile curve his lips.

"No. Really," he said when he saw hesitation in her eyes. "I was thinking about how there'd once been a time when I damn well wasn't willing to wait for what I wanted." The smile moved to his eyes. "Maybe I'm finally growing up. Or getting old." Now that was a depressing thought.

"You're certainly not old, Mitch," Tory assured him. She kept her eyes level with his, her tone matter-of-fact. "However, if you're referring to me, you've got a very long wait ahead of you. Like forever."

"Perhaps." He leaned back in his chair, lifted the cup of cooling coffee to his lips and eyed her over the rim. "Or perhaps not." His eyes gleamed with a teasing male confidence that Tory found both infinitely appealing and annoying.

Swearing under her breath, Tory bit into the croissant and began chewing furiously. It was buttery, flaky and the native nutmeg jam tasted like ambrosia, but she was too frustrated to appreciate it.

"Oh, Tory?" Mitch said casually.

She swallowed. "What now?"

His grin rivaled the bright La Paz sun. "You owe me fifty bucks."

"What?"

"The bet. You did spend the night with me, remember?"

"Not technically, I didn't. We didn't even sleep in the same room, Mitch Cantrell. Let alone in the same bed."

"Don't remind me."

Wrapping her braid around his hand, he tugged lightly, pulling her to him for a long, hard kiss that left no room for thought, let alone words. Her mouth softened, her head began to spin, a familiar, dangerous fire began to flicker inside her. She shouldn't want this, Tory warned herself. She shouldn't want it to go on and on and on.

"Next time," he said against her mouth as he prepared to release her, "we'll have to remedy that situation."

Emotions were clawing at her. She was shaking with anger and need and the fear that she'd already crossed some invisible line that would make retreat ultimately impossible.

"I've never met a man who could make me so angry." She stabbed a piece of papaya with her fork.

"That's the best news I've had all day."

The fork stopped halfway to her mouth. "What does that mean?"

His smile was vintage Mitch. "I'd hate to think that I bored you. Then we really would have a problem."

Before she could think of an answer, he stood up. "Better hurry and eat your breakfast, Victoria. Ramirez is scheduled back in town tomorrow and we have a lot of work to do. And a long drive ahead of us."

She knew it. He was bound and determined to take charge. The man was admittedly the best kisser she'd ever known—maybe even world champion—but she was damned if she was going to start taking orders from him as if she were playing Jimmy Olson or Lois Lane to his Superman.

"So where are we going?"

His answer immediately burst her little bubble of resistance. "The general's got a house in the mountains. Since only a handful of trusted people know about its existence, I'll bet that fifty dollars that you still owe me it's where we'll find out what's going on."

Anger changed to reluctant admiration. "I don't suppose you'd be willing to share how you found out about this place?"

"Now, Tory," Mitch said chidingly, "you know a good journalist—"

"Never reveals his sources," Tory finished with ill-concealed frustration.

"You always were a fast learner, Victoria Martin." Smiling, he reached out and pulled at the end of her braid in a friendly gesture. "Finish your breakfast. I'll be back in half an hour."

"Where are you going?"

"I've got a few things I need to take care of," he answered obliquely.

Something suddenly occurred to her. "There's no way we can get to the mountains and back in time for my performance tonight."

"I've already taken care of that."

Tory folded her arms. "I'm almost afraid to ask."

"It's no big deal. I simply called you in sick."

"What?"

"I called the manager, said I was your doctor, and told him that you were feeling ill and wouldn't be able to make tonight's performance."

"He's never going to believe that," Tory complained.

"Of course he will," Mitch assured her. "Especially after my old friend Dr. Mendoza confirms that you appear to be suffering from some stomach ailment, undoubtedly due to something you ate on the plane."

"So what will we do if the manager finds me gone?"

"I'm one step ahead of you. Mendoza is going to insist on taking you to his private clinic for treatment. We'll leave from there. In fact, the good doctor should be here in about forty-five minutes. So lock the door and don't answer it for anyone but me. Is that clear?"

"Really, Mitch," she protested, "I'm quite capable of taking care of myself."

He paused in the doorway and gave her a long hard look. "That remains to be seen," he said finally. "Lock this door."

With that he was gone, leaving Tory to wonder exactly when she'd lost control of the situation.

6

FOR A SMALL COUNTRY, La Paz was topographically very diverse. On the east coast, the near-tideless Caribbean Sea lapped against glistening white tropical sands, while on the west, the Pacific Ocean relentlessly pounded the rocky coastline. Inland from both coasts were steamy, sweltering alluvial lowlands and cool, high plateaus. A chain of lofty volcanic mountains marched north to south, forming a jagged backbone that effectively divided the country.

Mitch and Tory had left the Caribbean coast far behind them, driving through vast fields of bright tropical flowers and tobacco. They passed the banana plantations, where *segadores* harvested the still-green fruit with two swift swings of their razor-sharp machetes. The slopes rimming the central plateau were covered with coffee trees; the fragile-looking white flowers filled the air with a sweet, jasminelike fragrance.

Gradually the road narrowed and grew more winding, offering a dazzling view of pristine valleys and mighty rivers beneath an ever-changing sky. Although she was still irritated by Mitch's overbearing attitude, Tory couldn't help but admire the way he maneuvered the rented Jeep through the tight hairpin turns.

Moisture-laden clouds scudded overhead, casting long black shadows. The stand of primeval forest bordering the roadway appeared as dark and ominous as whispered rumors. In the distance Tory could see one of the country's eight active volcanoes—Volcán Monteverde—belching puffs of white smoke like an angry green giant.

As they crossed a wooden bridge, Tory looked a dizzying way down to the river below, where women, their skirts pulled up and tied to their hips, were beating clothes on rocks.

"It hasn't changed at all," she murmured, thinking back to the last time she'd been in this part of the country.

It had been two weeks before the fall of the ruthlessly corrupt government, fourteen days before General Ramirez would ride his captured government tank into the capital city to the enthusiastic cheers of his countrymen.

Rumors had circulated throughout the country that there had been an assassination attempt on the general; Ramirez, always cognizant of the value of good press relations, had called a news conference at one of his rebel camps in the mountains to prove that not only was he alive and well, but that all his men continued to be one hundred percent behind him.

"That's where we're going, isn't it?" she asked as they made the steep climb into the cloud forest. "To Monteverde."

Mitch nodded. "Very good. It's encouraging to discover you haven't lost your investigative instincts along with your common sense."

"I'm getting awfully tired of you accusing me of being stupid," she snapped.

"You've never been stupid, Tory," he remarked easily. A few fat drops of rain hit the windshield; Mitch turned on the wipers. "But you can't deny that your heart has an unfortunate tendency to overrule your head from time to time. And when it does, off you go, tilting at windmills again."

A convoy of army trucks passed, headed in the opposite direction filled with young, conscripted soldiers dressed in camouflage and holding carbines. Tory knew that the Ramirez government made routine raids on the mountain villages, rounding up any boy over fourteen years of age. The truck drivers arrogantly took up the center of the narrow roadway, forcing Mitch to pull over to the right. Just inches beyond the car's fender, the shoulder of the road sheared away. Tory shivered.

"I'd hardly call attempting to put the man who tried to kill my sister in prison tilting at windmills," she said.

"You can't deny that your personal involvement is making you act more rashly than you would under normal conditions," Mitch argued. He slanted her a quick look before returning his attention to his driving. "Is that what you want to do? Put the general behind bars?"

"If I did what I'd really like to do, the vice president would have another state funeral to attend and I'd be no better than Ramirez," Tory muttered. "So yes, since jail is the next best alternative, I'd like to see him put away forever."

"It wouldn't be enough just to have him lose the election?"

"No," she said quickly. Puzzled by his tone, Tory looked at him. "You couldn't possibly be thinking . . . ?

No. . . . Even you couldn't rig an election," she insisted. "Could you?"

"Who said anything about rigging it? There's always a chance the guy might lose honestly."

"But you said that the general had the election sewed up."

"That was last night," Mitch reminded her. "You know as well as I do that Central American politics is extremely fluid."

She stared at him, not quite trusting his casual, innocent attitude. "If someone were to attempt to tamper with the election, to turn the tide against Ramirez, and failed, that person could end up dead."

"I'd say there's a strong possibility of that."

Tory thought of her sister, of Amy's shattered face and broken bones. And then she thought of Mitch, lying dead in some dark Playa de Palma alley. Because of her.

"Mitch." Frightened, she put her hand upon his arm. "You're not thinking of doing anything crazy, are you?"

"Me?" The look he gave her was guileless. "Don't forget, Victoria, you're the one with the crazy plans. I'm simply trying to inject some reason into this low-budget thriller."

She wished she could believe him. But there was something he wasn't telling her. Something that made Tory wish she hadn't come to La Paz in the first place.

"You may be right," she said.

"About what?"

"I'm beginning to think perhaps I ought to drop this entire scheme and just go back to my real life. Where I maintain some semblance of control."

"It's too late for that, Tory."

"It's never too late."

"Now there's where you're wrong." This time his look was immeasurably serious and unnerving. "Because we both know that sometimes you don't have any choice but to see things through to the end."

From his solemn tone Tory had the feeling that they were no longer talking about her plan to bring down the general. Instead the conversation seemed to have taken a much more personal track. Not willing to tackle such an intimate topic now, while she was clinging to the edge of her seat, praying that they'd manage to reach Monteverde alive, Tory didn't answer.

The few random drops of water splashing onto the windshield turned into a drizzle. Then a steady rainfall. A thick mist rose to surround them and every so often Tory could see, illuminated in the headlights Mitch had turned on, barricades where the side of the road had washed away.

"How much farther?" she asked.

Mitch checked his watch. "Not much. Twenty, thirty minutes, if the weather holds." Mitch glance at her. "Nervous?"

"Of course not," Tory lied.

He chuckled, a low, deep appealing sound that had always possessed the power to thrill her. "Me neither. But I sure as hell will be glad when we get there." Reaching across the seat, he briefly, reassuringly, squeezed her hand.

Time spun backward; it was just like the old days. She and Mitch, together again, risking life and limb to track down a story. The thought made her smile.

The forest had grown so thick that Tory could no longer see the sky. The mist settled over the mountains, wrapping everything in a soft, silvery veil. The road passed through a tunnel, plunging them into a lengthy darkness as black and quiet as a tomb. The only light was the soft, fuzzy yellow glow of the car's headlights as they tried to penetrate the dark. Goose bumps rose on Tory's arms, but she kept her mouth clamped shut.

Mitch glanced at Tory once more, knowing that the tunnel could very well prove discomfiting. That shared night in the cave had taught him something about Tory he suspected very few individuals knew. She was afraid of the dark. The fear had been born the summer she was five, when she'd gotten lost while picking blackberries in the Wisconsin woods.

Although a search party had been formed the moment she was discovered missing, Tory had spent the night alone in the woods, huddled beneath a pine tree, listening to the sad, lonely cry of a coyote and the ominous rustling sounds of animals scurrying through the underbrush.

She really was something. Mitch watched her silently ball her hands into fists as the car entered a second tunnel. The other female foreign correspondents he'd met after Tory were every bit as hardworking as the men. They took risks and endured hardships that only an obsessed person would deem reasonable. But never had he met anyone—man or woman, for that matter—as fearless as the woman seated beside him.

"I used to love tunnels when I was a kid," he said.

Her head was spinning. It would pass, Tory assured herself as sweat beaded on her forehead. The dizziness, the nausea, the ice running through her veins.

Any moment they'd be out in the daylight again and she'd be fine. She took a deep breath.

"I always knew you were crazy," she muttered.

"It's not crazy," he argued easily, wanting to take her mind off the darkness that had blanketed them like a shroud. "When you're seven years old, it's exciting when your dad opens the car window and leans on the horn."

The car emerged from the blackness into the cloaking silvery mist. Breathing a sigh of relief, Tory shot him a glance, her deep-seated fear tempered by reluctant interest. "Why on earth would he do that?"

"I don't know. He just did."

"It sounds silly," she commented as they entered yet another tunnel.

He chuckled. "Some of the best things in life are." He took his right hand off the steering wheel long enough to trace the curve of her cheekbone with his finger. "Tell you what. On the way back down the mountain, we'll try it and you can decide for yourself."

His fleeting touch once again felt like a sparkler against her skin. Pleasure momentarily overcame dread, desire banished fear. Tory touched her own fingertips to her cheek, imagining that she could feel the heat even now.

"This is it," Mitch announced, turning off the main road onto one that was even narrower and more winding. After a series of increasingly tight curves, he pulled into a dense grove of broad-leaved evergreen trees. "The house is about three hundred yards due west."

Tory looked at the water rolling down the windshield. "I suppose we're going to have to walk." Although her tone was matter-of-fact, she couldn't conceal her lack of enthusiasm.

"I think we'd better," Mitch answered. "Unless you'd rather drive straight to the front gate and tell the guard that we're here looking for evidence to hang the general."

"There's a gate? And a guard?"

"Actually several. Guards, not gates," Mitch clarified. "As far as I know, there's only one way in or out."

"You didn't mention the guards back in Playa de Palma."

"Didn't I?"

"No."

He looked at her curiously. Maybe he'd taken too much for granted, Mitch thought. Perhaps, despite her crazy stunt posing as a torch singer, Tory had lost her appetite for adventure. "Would it have mattered?"

Tory only had to consider his question for a moment. "No," she said. "A few guards wouldn't have changed my mind."

Mitch let out the breath he'd been unaware of holding. She hadn't changed after all. Deciding that this wasn't the time to dwell on exactly why that had him feeling so good, Mitch reached into the back seat and pulled out a pair of hooded, drab green ponchos.

"I thought we might need these," he said, handing her one of the ponchos along with a pair of high rubber boots.

Tory pulled the lightweight waterproof poncho over her head. It was a great deal more comfortable than the old rubberized one she'd worn the last time she and Mitch had been in this forest. Even with the heavy outerwear, they'd gotten drenched before the general had finished his long-winded press conference.

Afterward they'd returned to the city, where Mitch had drawn her a rare hot bath filled to the brim with frothy bubbles, brought her a steaming mug of cappuccino and spent a long, luxurious time washing her back.

Later, after the bubbles had disappeared and the cappuccino was gone, he'd lifted her from the still-velvety water and carried her into the bedroom, where he'd proceeded to make her forget she'd ever been chilled.

The memory of that love-filled night made a flush rise into Tory's cheeks. When she risked a glance at Mitch, who was looking at her intently, she realized that once again they were on the same intimate wavelength.

He must have been insane to let this woman go, Mitch mused. Then again, Tory's charm had always been that she was so fiercely independent. *What makes you think you could have kept her, pal?* he asked himself grimly.

"Well, this rain doesn't look like it's going to let up," he said, dragging his eyes away to cast yet another quick glance at his watch.

The way he had been staring at her, Tory expected Mitch to say something profound or at least make another pass. When he didn't do either, she found herself strangely disappointed.

"No, it certainly doesn't, does it?" She looked glumly out at the slanting silver curtain.

"You could always stay here in the truck, while I check things out," Mitch suggested.

"And let you have all the fun?" Tory tugged on one boot. Then the other. "Not on your life, Cantrell." She opened the door. "Let's get this show on the road."

As they made their way toward the compound, Mitch was smiling.

THE GENERAL'S mountaintop home was surrounded by a chain-link fence topped with rolls of razor band. Inside the fence, armed men patrolled the perimeter, accompanied by guard dogs.

"It appears that you also forgot to mention the rottweilers," Tory hissed as they observed the compound from a distance.

Mitch checked his watch again. "I didn't forget. You didn't ask."

A blistering response came immediately to mind. Closing her eyes briefly to rein in her temper, Tory tried to remind herself that she'd entered into this adventure with her eyes wide open. "So now what?"

Before Mitch could answer, a low, rumbling sound like thunder echoed in the distance. "Right on time," he said.

As Tory watched, a large truck painted in camouflage green and brown lumbered up to the gate, which was immediately opened by one of the guards. The driver pulled the truck about fifty yards into the compound and stopped, whereupon a trio of soldiers, dressed in fatigues, exited the canvas-covered back.

"Mitch," Tory whispered excitedly, "those are U.S. soldiers."

"They seem to be," Mitch agreed.

Tory had worked with Mitch long enough to become immediately suspicious at the lack of surprise in his tone. "You knew they were coming here today, didn't you? That's why you kept looking at your watch."

"One of my sources mentioned that if I just happened to be at the right place at the right time today with my camera, I might discover something interesting," Mitch allowed. He watched as the soldiers grabbed a pile of canvas bags from the back of the truck.

Tory was watching through the binoculars Mitch had given her. As she focused on the bags, she saw that they were stenciled with the legend U. S. Army Mail.

"What do you suppose he's doing with those mailbags?" she murmured, her mind kicking into high gear as she attempted to put the pieces of the puzzle together.

Before Mitch could answer, another man exited the cab. As he glanced around the compound, Mitch viewed his face through the binoculars and breathed a low whistle.

"Do you know him?" Tory asked.

"Yeah. It's Colonel Warren Astor. He's a very ambitious man. General Howard, the base commander, is reportedly counting the days until his promotion to a cushy desk job at the Pentagon. Rumor also has it that Howard has developed a bit of a drinking problem of late. So, although he isn't the actual guy in charge, Astor has taken over as quasi commander."

While Mitch and Tory watched, the American soldiers made their way across the compound. They'd just reached the house when another man emerged and greeted the colonel with obvious enthusiasm.

Mitch nodded, pleased that he hadn't been sent out here on a wild-goose chase. "Bingo."

Tory glanced at him. "I take it you know him?"

"He's a Playa de Palma art dealer. He has more of a reputation for false passports than scruples."

A piece of the puzzle fell into place. "He's smuggling artifacts." Even during her time in the country eight years ago, the demand for pre-Columbian archaeological treasures had reached epidemic proportions. The plundering of ancient sites was normally done by gangs of locals who passed their finds to unscrupulous agents, who in turn forwarded them to dealers in New York and Miami, as well as Brussels, Zurich and other foreign cities.

"I'd say that's a pretty good guess," Mitch agreed.

"And they're using the army mail to bypass customs."

"Could be."

Tory shot him an accusing look. "You knew all about this, didn't you? That's why you refused to accept my theory that Ramirez was smuggling drugs."

"Let's just say that I ran across rumors while I was in Colombia," Mitch said.

"So you came down here to investigate. You didn't leave because of the drug lords' death threats at all." Tory didn't know whether to admire him or be amazed that after all he'd been through, he was still willing to risk his life for a story.

"I'm not the kind of guy to let threats scare me off a story, Tory," Mitch said quietly. "You of all people should understand that."

Yes, she did. But for some reason she was not going to attempt to understand now, Tory found herself wishing he'd use a bit more caution. He was, she concluded, still the same, full-steam-ahead man she'd fallen in love with.

"I doubt that General Howard would be very receptive to the idea that his second in command is running a smuggling ring," Tory mused, turning her thoughts back to the problem at hand.

"It might tend to screw up his promotion," Mitch agreed. "Since people would have to wonder how such a thing could be going on right under the base commander's nose." When the colonel disappeared into the house, Mitch lowered the binoculars and rubbed the bridge of his nose. "Besides, even if we could find out what's in those bags and pin a smuggling rap on the colonel, that doesn't solve your personal dilemma concerning Ramirez."

"What are you talking about?" Impatient, Tory turned on him. "This is his house. Of course he's involved in whatever is going on in there."

"You know that and I know that," Mitch said. "But it doesn't prove a thing."

"Dammit, Mitch—" Furious, she raised her voice— just enough to garner attention from one of the dogs. It suddenly turned in their direction, ears pricked to attention.

"Terrific," Mitch whispered. "Whatever you do, don't move. Or breathe."

They remained statue still. As the rottweiler approached the fence, blood was pounding in Tory's ears, louder and louder, like something from one of Edgar Allan Poe's horror stories. When the dog began to bark, her blood turned to ice.

Two guards approached the fence, one bringing another dog who joined in the raucous barking. The men began talking in rapid-fire Spanish that could not be overheard over the sound of the dogs. Mitch knew that if he raised the binoculars in an attempt to read the men's lips, there'd be a risk of light shining off the lenses. For now, all he could do was to hold tight to Tory's icy hand and hope for the best.

"If they start to come this way," he said out of the side of his mouth, "I want you to run like hell back to the truck and drive down the mountain. Don't stop until you get back to the city."

"What about you? What will you be doing while I'm running away?" Tory whispered.

Some things never changed, Mitch decided grimly. Including the fact that this woman would probably argue with Saint Peter. "Dammit, don't worry about me. I'll be fine."

Sure. Who did he think he was? Tory wondered as she took in the snarling, barking dogs and the automatic rifles the guards carried. Superman?

"I'm not leaving you."

Mitch took one look at her tilted chin and bit back a harsh oath. One of these days, he and Tory Martin were going to have a long, serious discussion about feminine acquiescence. But right now, as he watched the dogs straining at their leashes, choke chains tightening around their thick necks, Mitch was preoccupied with getting Tory and himself out of here alive. Once they were safely back in the city, he was going to give Tory holy hell.

The soldiers' actions spoke louder than words as they approached the gate, obviously planning to release the rottweilers, allowing them to attack their prey. Men in the house, alerted by the noise, had come outside too, weapons drawn, to join the guards in the compound.

Just when Mitch was beginning to think that his luck had finally run out, there was a sudden loud squealing sound nearby. As he and Tory watched, a pig, probably belonging to some campesino living in the area, tore out of the bushes, headed toward the fence. The dogs went wild. A moment later a jaguar appeared and in two long graceful strides caught the pig by the neck. As the sleek beast dragged its prey back into the forest, the soldiers visibly relaxed and began to laugh.

Mitch and Tory let out their breath in unison.

"I never thought I'd be relieved to run across a jaguar in the wild," she whispered shakily.

Mitch, agreeing wholeheartedly, squeezed her hand.

Inside the compound things returned to normal. When one of the dogs continued to bark, a guard gave him a swift kick in the ribs, effectively silencing him immediately.

A short time later, the U.S. soldiers emerged from the house with their mailbags bulging. "From the weight of those bags, I doubt if they're taking airmail letters back to the States," Mitch observed. They watched the soldiers stow the heavy bags in the back of the truck.

"Now what?" Tory asked as the truck lumbered through the gate.

"Now that we've discovered what Ramirez is up to, I say we get out of here," Mitch suggested. "Before those rottweilers decide we've overstayed our welcome."

They followed the army truck at a discreet distance for approximately forty-five minutes. They were passing through a village of unpainted houses topped with flat tin roofs covered with rust, when the truck suddenly pulled off the curving road and parked in front of a weather-beaten cantina perched precariously on the edge of the cliff.

"Mitch," Tory complained, grabbing his arm when he continued driving past the cantina, "we have to stop."

"No, we don't."

"But they're probably going to meet Ramirez."

Mitch glanced into the outside rearview mirror, took one look at the armed soldiers emerging from the truck and decided that it was time Tory learned that she couldn't always have things her way. "The general's in the central valley."

"He was yesterday. Who knows where he is today? Besides, they're obviously stopping for some reason."

"Maybe they're hungry. Or thirsty." He knew *he* could certainly do with a beer about now. Ever since those rottweilers had apparently spotted them, Mitch's mouth had been as dry as the Sahara.

"And maybe they're meeting another member of their gang. Maybe they're going to hand the goods over to someone else. You have to stop, Mitch. Now! Or I'll take the keys out of the ignition."

She would, too, Mitch knew. One thing about Tory Martin, she was not a woman to make idle threats. Cursing softly, he pulled to the side of the road and cut the ignition. When Tory looked inclined to grab the keys anyway, he slipped them into his pocket.

"Look," he said, struggling for patience, "since the stuff is in the U.S. army mailbags, it only makes sense that they're going to take it back to the base and incor-

porate it into the next planeload of mail going out to the
States."

"You don't know that for certain," Tory retorted,
unwilling to admit that he had a very good point. Although she was honestly grateful for Mitch's help,
which she had to admit was speeding up her investigation, she was getting very tired of him calling all the
shots.

The back and forth motion of his jaw suggested that
Mitch was grinding his teeth. "No, I don't," he agreed.
"But it's a logical assumption."

Tory folded her arms. "I don't remember you relying
on assumptions, logical or not, when you went on the
air with a story. In fact, the Mitchell Cantrell I used to
know and respect was renowned for never having to
retract a statement. Because he always triple-checked
his sources." She smiled sweetly. "But of course, that
was a long time ago and I understand how things can
change. How people change."

He'd gotten her point, loud and clear. If she thought
that five years of captivity in Lebanon had made him
soft, or even worse, lazy, the lady definitely had a great
deal to learn.

Mitch's gaze locked on hers. "I have every intention
of checking the colonel out as soon as we get back to
the city. Which is why," he grunted, "I can't see any
point in wasting time by stopping."

A lesser woman would have been intimidated by his
glare, but Tory met his look, as intense as he. "And I
don't want to take a chance on missing something important. Now, are you going to turn this Jeep around,
or shall I just get out and walk back to the cantina?"

She was either every bit as reckless as ever or certifiably crazy. Although Mitch couldn't quite decide which, the one thing he was certain of was that when all this was over, he was going to lay down the law. The only problem was, he hadn't quite decided how to make it stick.

He dug his hands into his pocket and pulled out the keys. "Dammit, Victoria..."

Encouraged when he jammed the key into the ignition, Tory opted to ignore his savage look. "Does this mean you're going back?"

"Do I have any choice?"

"You always have a choice," she told him, reminding him of his own words. Now that she'd gotten her way, she could afford to be gracious. "Thank you, Mitch."

He twisted the key, bringing the engine to life. "Save your thanks," he muttered, making a U-turn and heading back in the direction of the cantina. "At least until we get out of that damn place alive."

"You don't have to worry," she assured him. "After all, what harm can there be in two people going into a cantina for a tall cool beer?"

There could be tons of harm when the other patrons of that cantina just happened to be members of an international smuggling ring, Mitch reasoned grimly. For an intelligent woman, Tory Martin really could be an idiot.

But, he decided, thinking of the way she'd felt in his arms last night, she was a rather sweet idiot.

Actually that wasn't really true either, Mitch amended as he pulled into the dirt lot and parked beside a battered school bus, its top piled high with gunnysacks and boxes. There was nothing lacking in Tory's brainpower. What got her into trouble was her unwavering loyalty—to people and to causes.

The fact that she loved her younger sister was obvious. That she was willing to risk her own life to avenge Amy was also, unfortunately, all too obvious. So there was nothing Mitch could do to stop her short of making good his threat to tie her up and toss her onto the first plane to the States. The only problem with his scenario was that she'd probably get loose and be back on the trail before the damn plane managed to clear the runway.

"You leave all the talking to me," he warned as they left the Jeep. "This is no place for you to play James Bond."

"I wasn't going to do any such thing," she snapped. "For Pete's sake, Mitchell Cantrell, I'm not totally lacking in common sense."

"You sure as hell could have fooled me."

As he slammed the truck door behind him, Mitch found himself thinking that they could have spent the day lying on the beach, feeding each other succulent tropical fruits and making love. But no, instead he'd embarked on a fool's expedition that could very well end up getting them killed.

Insanity was obviously contagious.

What was even worse was the realization that for the first time in a very long while—six years to be exact— he was actually enjoying himself.

7

THE INSIDE of the cantina reminded Tory of something from the late, late show. In black and white, she decided. This shack would never rate Technicolor. The unpainted adobe walls were caked with what looked to be a century's worth of dirt, the floor was covered with sawdust, which Tory assumed had once been a nice, bright yellow, but now was the color of soot.

The scent of cigarette smoke, spilled beer and mildew hovered over the room like an oppressive cloud, while a rusty paddle-bladed fan overhead creaked in a futile attempt to move the moist air. A grizzled campesino, wearing a ragged straw hat, sat by the door, tossing back shots of tequila. Three women with eyes far older than their years sat atop bar stools. They were obviously working girls, dressed for the evening in bright polka dot dresses, red lipstick and skyscraper-high heels.

"What a dump," she said under her breath.

Under usual conditions, Tory's Bette Davis impression would have made Mitch smile. But as his gaze slowly circled the room, he couldn't find anything remotely humorous about either their location or their situation.

"I'm ready to leave whenever you are," he offered.

Through the thick blue haze Tory viewed the colonel, seated with his men at a table in the corner. "Not on your life, Cantrell." After carefully checking out the seat, she sat down on the edge of a rickety chair at a nearby table.

"Why don't you get us something to drink?" she suggested brightly. "I think I'd like a *cerveza*. In the bottle," she added, eyeing the dingy, greasy glass left on the neighboring table by an earlier patron.

"Finally," Mitch said dryly, "a sensible suggestion."

Tory had two choices. She could be offended by his sarcasm, or she could simply ignore it for the sake of peace. She opted for the latter. "How nice of you to say so," she said sweetly.

Shaking his head with building frustration, Mitch went over to the scarred bar and ordered the drinks from an overweight bartender who looked as if he'd escaped from a chain gang. His eyes were the flat, unsmiling orbs of a Gila monster, his oily black hair hung to his bulldog shoulders, a jagged red scar bisected his cheek and his bulky arms, which reminded Mitch of hams, were covered in a garish display of red and blue tattoos.

The tattoo artist's favorite theme, Mitch observed as the bartender slammed the two dark green bottles onto the bar, seemed to be snakes. There was a dizzying display of the scaly reptiles posed in strike position along with a random scorpion, and a jaguar that was stalking its way up the man's left forearm.

"*¡Gracias!*" Mitch said, not surprised when he received no reply. Then out of the blue a spark of interest flickered in the flat dark eyes. Following the bartender's gaze, Mitch had to stifle his groan when he saw that Tory had taken off her poncho, immediately garnering the attention of every man in the place.

He was on the way back to the table, a beer in each hand, when the colonel suddenly appeared in front of him. "I thought that was you, Cantrell," Astor said in a big, booming voice clearly accustomed to barking out orders. "What the hell brings you out to this godforsaken neck of the woods?"

When the colonel's smile didn't quite reach his slate-gray eyes, Mitch realized the man was suspicious. Which wasn't all that surprising. If he were sitting on a truckload of hot pre-Columbian treasures, he'd probably get a little uptight if a reporter suddenly appeared on the scene.

"Good afternoon, Colonel," Mitch greeted the officer. "We're just out on a little sight-seeing expedition."

"Rotten day for sight-seeing," the colonel pointed out.

"The weather was bright and sunny in the city when we left," Mitch argued easily. "I guess I forgot how temperamental the climate can be up in these mountains."

"Yet you certainly came prepared," the colonel noted, his gaze taking in Mitch's poncho and boots.

Mitch grinned. "I used to be a Boy Scout."

The colonel digested that for a long, heart-stopping minute before turning his attention to Tory. "Who's your lady friend?"

"Laura Winter," Mitch improvised without missing a beat.

The colonel rubbed his square jaw. "The name doesn't ring a bell. Is she with the network?"

"Oh, no sir," Mitch hastened to assure him. If one foreign correspondent was all it took to set off the colonel's internal alarm, he didn't want to contemplate

what the man might make of two reporters coinciden-
tally showing up in the same cantina. "Laura's a sec-
retary at the embassy."

Mitch could see the colonel relax. "She's quite striking," the officer said with obvious interest. "I'd like to
meet her."

Mitch, who would just as soon have introduced Tory
to Count Dracula, vowed that once he got her out of
here, he was never again going to give in to any of her
stupid, dangerous demands. "I'm sure she'd enjoy
meeting you, sir."

Tory had been watching the exchange with interest
and drew in a quick breath when Mitch returned to the
table with the colonel in tow.

"Laura," he said, "I'd like you to meet Colonel Astor. The colonel is second in command at the base.
Colonel, Laura Winter."

Tory held out her hand. "Hello, Colonel," she said,
offering him a smile that was just a degree less inviting
than La Rubia's famous one. "You have no idea what a
pleasure this is. Ah've heard ever so much about you."
Her voice was softened with a sugary drawl that
brought to mind long, lazy summer afternoons in the
antebellum South.

Dammit, she was doing it again, Mitch considered
darkly. Diving headfirst into dangerous waters without first bothering to check the depth. Mitch had heard
Tory's Southern belle routine before. The last time had
been immediately after the coup, when she'd coaxed
one of Ramirez's disillusioned cabinet members into
leaking the general's intention of taking absolute control of the government. At the time Mitch had warned
her that such a blatantly sexual ploy could be danger-

ous; Tory, in turn, had calmly pointed out that it had worked. She'd gotten her story, hadn't she? One that succeeded in winning a Pulitzer prize nomination.

The colonel enveloped Tory's slender hand in his much larger one. "On the contrary, Miss Winter, the pleasure is all mine." When Tory would have tugged her hand loose, his fingers tightened ever so slightly, effectively holding her hand hostage. "As I was telling Cantrell, you are very lovely."

Ignoring Mitch's blistering look, Tory blushed on cue. "Why, thank you, Colonel. That's a very sweet thing to say."

"It's the truth," Astor insisted. "Which is why I wonder why we've never met before. I spend a great deal of time at the embassy and I know I haven't seen you."

"Ah've only been in La Paz a short time. But Ah've certainly heard good things about you, Colonel," she said, offering him yet another smile even as she made a subtle attempt to retrieve her hand once again. "The scuttlebutt about the embassy is that you are about to be promoted to base commander."

Her eyes filled with admiration laced with just the appropriate amount of awe. "In fact, people say that since you're already the actin' commander, your promotion will merely acknowledge the excellent work you've been doin' here in La Paz."

Colonel Warren Astor was a hard-boiled career officer in his fifties. The graduate of West Point was also a throwback to another, long-ago time, when men couldn't wait to march off to fight in glorious wars. During his terms in both Korea and Vietnam, he'd been awarded nearly every medal his country could bestow upon an American soldier.

He'd killed more men than he could count and he'd watched his own men die. If anyone had dared tell him that the young soldiers under his command feared him, he would have answered that they damn well better. He was what was once referred to as a man's man. But that didn't mean that the colonel wasn't as susceptible to feminine flattery as the next guy.

Astor turned toward Mitch. "Your lady's intelligent as well as beautiful."

Mitch nodded. "She has her moments."

"I'll just bet she does." The colonel took a long, leisurely tour of Tory's face. "You're a lucky man."

"I try to remind myself of that several times a day," Mitch said.

Tory didn't like the way the men were talking about her as if she weren't there. And the way they were looking at her made her feel like a prize cocker spaniel at the Westminster dog show.

"Didn't you say something about havin' to make a phone call, sugah?" she asked Mitch.

Irritation flickered in his eyes, but Mitch quickly doused it. "It can wait."

The one thing he didn't want to do was leave Tory alone with Astor. The way the guy was looking at her— as if he were a starving man and she his private smorgasbord—was less than encouraging. Add to that Tory's tendency to be a loose cannon, and the situation was rife with explosive possibilities.

"If you're worried about leavin' me alone, Ah'm sure the colonel will be willing to keep me company," she insisted. Pulling out all the stops, she graced Astor with her most dazzling La Rubia smile.

"I'd be honored to watch over your lady, Cantrell," Astor assured Mitch. "Although it must be an important phone call," he suggested, "if it can't wait until you get back to the city."

Mitch viewed the renewed suspicion flickering in those slate-gray eyes and worried once again about leaving Tory with so perceptive an enemy. The colonel hadn't gotten where he was by being naive. Or stupid.

"I promised my producer I'd check in," he said. "With the election so close, he wasn't wild about me taking the afternoon off."

The colonel gave him a long, intense look. Then, apparently deciding that Mitch posed no threat, he smiled. "It's obvious that your producer hasn't met Ms. Winter," he said. "If he had, he certainly would have understood why the idea of a day in the country was far preferable to covering another election. Especially one as cut-and-dried as this one is going to be.

"Go make your call, Cantrell," he instructed, waving toward a pay phone hanging on the wall. "Miss Winter will be safe with me."

Sure. About as safe as a declawed kitten in a nest of pit vipers, Mitch considered darkly. If she could only keep her mouth shut for once . . . Giving Tory one last warning look, he had no choice but to leave her alone with the colonel.

Astor immediately claimed the chair beside her. "You know," he said reflectively, "the older I get, the more I realize that life is filled with coincidence."

Now that she was actually alone with the man, Tory found herself more than a little unnerved by the gleam in his eyes. "Oh?" Feigning an equanimity she was a long way from feeling, she lifted the bottle to her lips and took a drink.

"You work at the embassy," he explained. He pulled a long dark cigar out of his pocket, sniffed it appreciatively, clipped the end, then lighted it. "And I'm invited to the ambassador's reception for La Rubia."

Tory merely nodded. Knowing where this was going, she didn't want to offer the man any encouragement. Instead she began tracing with her fingernail the names carved onto the scarred wooden tabletop. Tony loved María, Angel loved Lupe, Manuel loved Eleana, who in turn professed to love José. Juanita, she noticed, was the wild card in the bunch. The seemingly practical woman loved two things: men and money.

"Perhaps I'll see you there," Astor suggested after a long pause, during which time Tory had remained stubbornly silent.

She smiled an apology. "Ah'm afraid Ah won't be goin'."

"Why not? It's sure to be the social event of the season."

As he began puffing away at the cigar, the resultant clouds of smoke reminded Tory of the smoke and ash routinely sent skyward by Volcán Monteverde. In his own way, the colonel could be every bit as dangerous as the still-active volcano.

"That's just it," she stressed earnestly. "Everyone in Playa de Palma has been tryin' to get an invitation to the reception, and Ah should know, because Ah've taken hundreds of the calls myself," she improvised blithely. "So with tickets at such a premium, there isn't any place for a mere civil servant on the ambassador's A list."

"You are much more than a mere civil servant, my dear." The colonel reached out and patted her hand. "Perhaps I could speak to the ambassador," he suggested significantly. "I am, after all, not without influence."

Tory forced yet another smile. "You've no idea how much Ah appreciate your offer, Colonel," she said. "But the truth is, Ah've made other plans for the evening."

His frown sent his shaggy, pewter-gray eyebrows diving toward his nose, making Tory decide that the colonel was definitely not accustomed to taking no for an answer. "Really? I would have guessed that as a member of the esteemed fourth estate, Cantrell will be attending the reception."

She nodded, realizing that she was in danger of getting herself into quicksand the longer this conversation continued. "Ah'm sure he is," she agreed. "But mah plans for the evening did not include Mitchell."

The colonel studied the glowing end of his cigar as he considered her words. "Then you and Cantrell aren't an item?"

"We're good friends," she answered. "But that's all."

"I see." Obviously pleased by that idea, he leaned back in the chair and resumed puffing on the cigar. "Perhaps you could break your previous engagement," he suggested.

"Ah'm afraid I couldn't do that, Colonel."

"But I'll miss you."

Tory knew that Astor wanted her at that party. And what the colonel wanted, the colonel undoubtedly got. She wondered what he would say if she told him that there was no way both Laura Winter and La Rubia could possibly show up at the same reception.

"Don't you worry, Colonel. Why, I'm sure that as soon as La Rubia arrives, Ah won't be missed."

When the colonel looked inclined to argue, Tory's sudden sneeze put him off.

"Gracious, Ah'm sorry," she said, sniffling inelegantly as she dug into her pocket for a tissue. When she couldn't find one, the colonel handed her a large white linen square with his initials embroidered in one corner. "Thank you," she gasped as she sneezed again. And again.

The sneezes continued, forestalling all further conversation until the colonel turned back toward the other table, where his men had now been joined by the trio of buxom women. "Walker," he barked, "bring me that box of Kleenex from the truck."

To his credit, the uniformed man's obvious aversion to going out into the pouring rain lasted no more than a heartbeat. "Yessir," he responded.

Pushing back from the table, he stood up so abruptly that his wooden chair—a duplicate of Tory's wobbly one—tipped over, clattering onto the sawdust-covered floor. The sudden sound caused a furry black spider the size of Tory's fist to scuttle across the room and up the screen door, where it disappeared through a gaping hole in the black mesh.

"This is so embarrassing," Tory managed between bouts of sneezing.

"Don't think anything of it, my dear," the colonel insisted. "I often suffer the same thing this time of year. The coffee blossoms," he elaborated. "Those damn innocuous-looking white flowers are murder on my sinuses. That's why I never travel without an adequate supply of Kleenex. Speaking of which—" he glared at the door "—what the hell is keeping Walker?"

At that moment the soldier returned, drenched from the waist down. He was protecting the box of tissue inside his camouflage poncho as if it were the Dead Sea scrolls. "Here you are, sir," he said, practically coming to attention as he reached the table.

"Don't give them to me, Walker," the colonel growled as Tory started sneezing yet again. "Can't you see it's Ms. Winter who needs them?"

"Yessir." The young man extended the plastic box across the table. "Here you are, ma'am."

"Thank you." Tory accepted the box, pulled out a white tissue and began dabbing at her eyes, which weren't being helped by the rank cloud of cigar smoke that had settled over their table. "Ah do so appreciate you goin' back out in that horrid weather, Mr. Walker."

"No problem, ma'am," the young man insisted, looking at Tory in a way that assured her he found her more than a little attractive, even with watery eyes and a red nose. "Besides, the rain is beginning to let up."

Tory blew her nose. "It's still quite considerate," she said. "It's so nice to know that chivalry isn't dead. Even out here in the end of nowhere."

The colonel had obviously decided that the wrong person was earning credit here. "That's enough, Walker," he growled. "You can rejoin the others."

The young man's gaze moved from Tory to the table where his friends were laughing with the women, then back to Tory again. It was obvious that he was comparing the women. It was also more than a little obvious that he much preferred Tory.

"Walker." The colonel's voice was a low, rumbling warning, once again reminding Tory of a volcano about to erupt.

"Yessir." The man snapped a salute, gave Tory one final yearning look and walked back across the room.

Tory blew her nose again, relieved that the sneezes seemed to have abated. It wasn't easy being sexy and appealing when your nose was running, she decided, wondering if Mata Hari had ever experienced these petty little problems.

"Gracious, Ah didn't know the army had regulation tissue boxes." She studied the brown and green plastic box with interest.

"It all boils down to image," Astor told her between puffs on the cigar. "Soldiers are fighting men. Trained killers. Think how it would look for us to be caught carrying floral boxes filled with pastel floral tissues."

"It'd undoubtedly signal the downfall of American military supremacy," Mitch said dryly as he rejoined them at the table.

The colonel frowned and ran his hand over his gray crew cut. "You liberal left-wing antiestablishment press types are all the same," he muttered. "If you had your way, we'd all be speaking Russian and eating borscht instead of watching the demise of communism."

Mitch glanced at Tory. "Take a good look," he invited. "Because you're looking at an endangered species. The last of the cold warriors."

"And damn proud of it," Astor returned shortly.

"Well, Ah for one am sincerely grateful for the army's presence in La Paz," Tory said, fluttering her dark lashes in a way that Scarlett O'Hara would have envied.

"Why, just knowing that so many brave men are nearby makes me feel ever so much safer."

"Thank you, little lady." The colonel patted her hand. "It's nice to know that you don't let your boyfriend do all your thinking for you."

Tory exchanged a look with Mitch. "On the contrary, Colonel," she said sweetly. "Ah have always known my own mind."

"And she's never been afraid to speak it, either," Mitch muttered.

"I like that in a woman," the colonel declared. "So long as she doesn't get carried away, of course."

Tory placed her elbows on the scarred table, cupped her chin in her hands and met his eyes with a cool, unblinking gaze. "What exactly do you consider getting carried away, Colonel?" she questioned in a deceptively quiet tone that Mitch had learned to recognize. During their brief, tempestuous affair, he'd heard it too many times to count. Usually right before she started throwing things.

"You know." The colonel lifted his shoulders in a shrug. "One of those *me-too* women."

"*Me-too* women?" Tory repeated, her voice rising dangerously. Mitch moved the dark green bottle safely out of range.

"The ones who make the mistake of thinking that anything a man can do, they can do, too," Astor explained.

Tory nodded slowly. "Ah see. Ah suppose that you are referring specifically to women in the military?"

"Exactly. That's a perfect case." From his obvious relief that she'd understood his point so quickly, Tory had the feeling that the colonel had been involved in his share of arguments concerning women's equality. "As a career soldier, I've seen those government bureaucrats in Washington screw up a lot of things, but never have I seen anything as asinine as putting a military uniform on a woman, handing her a gun and expecting her to step up to the front line.

"I mean, give me a break—" he was obviously warming to his subject "—when the going gets rough, no red-blooded American soldier wants a female hunkered down in the foxhole with him."

"Ah have difficulty believing that the average American male's sense of manhood is quite as fragile as you're suggesting, Colonel," Tory pointed out.

It was obvious that the colonel was not used to having his opinions questioned. Especially by a mere woman. "Hell, we're not talking about an ego thing, here, little lady," Astor retorted. "What we're talking about is the ability to save your buddy, if necessary, in the middle of a firefight. And a woman is simply not physically or psychologically capable of holding up her end of the stick."

"Excuse me, Colonel, but the picture you're paintin' is that of the farmer putting down his plow, shoulderin' a rifle and marchin' off to fight for God and country."

The man's eyes narrowed. "Something wrong with that?"

"Only that it's totally out of date." Forgetting her plan to charm the colonel, Tory began to get really wound up. Having experienced numerous instances of sexual discrimination in her professional life, she felt a personal responsibility to women everywhere to strike out at such behavior whenever it reared its ugly head.

"That patriotic red, white and blue image may have had some basis in reality a hundred years ago, but even as far back as World War II, military manpower specialists at the Pentagon admitted that half the men in uniform were doing jobs that could have been done equally as well by a woman."

"That's bull," Astor growled.

"That's the truth, Colonel," Tory snapped back.

Mitch watched the danger flags wave in Tory's cheeks and decided that they were about two minutes from all-out war. "I'm sorry to have to cut short such a stimulating conversation." Curving his long fingers firmly around Tory's elbow, he practically yanked her out of her chair. "But I really do have to get back to the city. There are rumors of street demonstrations and my producer wants me there, just in case."

"Really, Mitch," Tory protested, "can't someone else cover any demonstrations?"

"Not as well as I can," he answered. Turning toward the colonel, he lifted his right hand in a mock salute. "Always good to see you, sir."

Astor's answer was a muttered grunt. Then, turning to Tory, he said, "You know, little lady, I have this sneaking feeling that you're one of those feminist agitators."

"Oh, you do, do you?"

"Yes Ma'am, you're a real firebrand, Laura Winter, but on you it looks pretty good," Astor allowed. "I've always liked a gal with spunk." He winked. "Makes things more interesting, if you know what I mean."

"Ah believe Ah'm gettin' the idea," Tory replied. When her hand curled into a fist at her side, Mitch decided that it was past time to leave.

"Come on, sweetheart," he said, stuffing her poncho into her arms. "You wouldn't want me to lose my job now, would you?"

"I don't know who I'm madder at," Tory fumed as she marched toward the Jeep. "You or that jarheaded military throwback to the Dark Ages."

"Jarheads are marines," Mitch pointed out as he unlocked the passenger door. The rain had subsided to a light, cooling mist. "Astor's regular army. But he is a little behind the times."

Standing behind Tory as she climbed into the high seat, Mitch decided, not for the first time, that she had the nicest little bottom he'd ever seen packed into a pair of jeans. And even knowing that she'd consider such a thought outrageously chauvinistic didn't change his mind.

"Behind the times?" Tory repeated scathingly as he joined her in the front seat of the Jeep. "That idiot would make a Neanderthal look like Phil Donahue."

"I take it you didn't much take to the guy."

"Let's just say that I'll enjoy watching him march off to federal prison," she told him, gritting her teeth. "Where he can spend the next twenty to fifty years in the company of the overly macho type of man he so admires."

"At least it's nice to know that you're not vindictive."

Tory glared suspiciously at Mitch as he backed the Jeep out of the parking lot. "Are you laughing at me?"

"Me? Never."

"Good. Because I'm equally as furious with you."

"So you said. What exactly did I do now?"

"How about dragging me out of that cantina like some disobedient German shepherd?" she challenged. "In case you've forgotten, Cantrell, the plan was to stake out the cantina until we discovered who Astor was meeting."

"That was your plan," he reminded her. "Not mine. And from what I overheard those soldiers saying, the only meeting Astor is planning for tonight is going to involve those young ladies of the evening. And for the record, Victoria, German shepherds are never disobedient. I think it's somehow bred into their genes."

"That's ridiculous."

"Tory, Tory." He clicked his tongue. "Didn't you ever watch Rin Tin Tin when you were a kid?"

Tory wanted to stay mad at him. Really she did. But it was hard to hold a grudge against a man whose smile could warm you to the core. "Speaking of jeans," she muttered, rubbing her palms over the wet denim encasing her legs, "I wish you'd thought to toss in some waterproof pants while you were at it. I'm drenched from the knees down. I'm probably going to catch pneumonia."

"Don't worry. When we get back to my house, I'll be more than happy to warm you up."

The seductive promise was there, just waiting for Tory to pick up on it. She decided that she'd played with enough fire for one day.

"Thanks, anyway," she said, dragging her eyes away from his smiling blue ones to the side of the road, where two boys were driving a gaily painted ox cart. "But after we develop those pictures you took of Astor carrying the plundered loot out to that military truck and formulate the next step of our plan, all I want is a hot bath, a good meal and a soft bed. In that order."

"Sounds like a good idea," Mitch agreed. "Especially the part about the soft bed."

"Alone," Tory amended firmly.

"You'll like my bed," he assured her. "It's got goose-down pillows."

Tory sniffed. "I hate goose-down. It makes me sneeze."

"So we'll improvise and make love in the tub. How long can you hold your breath?"

"Probably a great deal longer than you'd need."

Mitch grimaced. "Ouch."

"If you can't stand the heat . . ." Tory suggested with a false, sweet smile.

"You're just lucky that I'm a sucker for a woman with an attitude," Mitch said. "You know, the colonel was definitely right about one thing."

"What?"

"That for a card-carrying feminist, you really are kind of cute when you're riled."

Tory bristled right on cue. "Talk about your sexist—"

Mitch cut her off. "I don't suppose you'd change your mind about the sleeping arrangements if I told you that I'd been fantasizing making love to you for a very long time?"

Tory folded her arms over her chest and wondered if he actually thought she'd just fallen off the back of a banana truck. She'd heard some imaginative lines in her day, and some of the best had come from Mitchell Cantrell, but there was no way she was going to buy this one.

"I'd say you ought to try selling that bridge to someone else. I've told you before, Mitch, I have no intention of picking up our affair where we left off. And even if I believe you, which I don't, that story still wouldn't be enough to make me change my mind."

Mitch gave her a long look. "You're positive about that?"

Tory nodded. "Absolutely."

Mitch shrugged. "Okay."

She knew him well enough not to trust him when he turned so agreeable. "We're simply two reporters, working together on a story," she insisted.

"Fine."

"After all, we're both intelligent people."

"I like to think at least one of us is," Mitch agreed. Tory's answering glare earned her a boyish grin. "Okay, both of us."

He'd always been an expert at baiting her, Tory considered. He'd always known exactly what strings to pull to make her temper flare. Just as he'd always known exactly what buttons to push to make her body burn.

"And intelligent people don't keep making the same mistakes over and over again," she said.

"I'm not certain I appreciate being referred to as a mistake," Mitch murmured.

"You know what I mean. We are not going to have an affair, Mitch. And that's final." Her words sounded false, even to her own ears, but Tory was not about to back down on this all-important issue. Mitch had already garnered too much power over their situation; she was damned if she was going to give him sexual control as well.

Mitch wondered if Tory honestly believed that they were capable of a strictly professional relationship and decided that deep down inside, where it counted, she probably didn't. But since he could also divine that for some unfathomable female reason it was important for her to believe that things could remain platonic between them, he'd allow her to pretend indifference. For now.

There simply wasn't any point in forcing the issue, he told himself. She wouldn't be able to resist the chemistry between them forever.

In the meantime, his years of captivity had taught him patience. Oh, he still didn't like it. But as he imagined burying himself in the silky-warm feminine sheath of her body, Mitch forced himself to remember that some things—and some women—were worth waiting for.

"Hey, it's your call. But if you change your mind and decide that you do want my magnificent male body, after all, you're going to have to make the first move. Because from now on, this reporter's going to be on his best behavior."

Tory arched a slender, disbelieving brow. "I suppose you expect me to believe that? After the way you've been trying to seduce me ever since my arrival in La Paz?"

Mitch lifted his right hand in a gesture of a pledge. "On my honor, Victoria. You're as safe with me as you'd be with your own brother."

"I don't have a brother."

Did the woman have to argue every little point? "I was merely speaking hypothetically."

"Oh. That's better."

Tory knew that Mitch was a man of his word. If he promised that he wasn't going to try to make love to her again, he'd live up to that promise, even if it wasn't his first choice.

Even as she told herself she should be relieved by this new declaration, Tory found herself feeling strangely depressed.

8

MITCH'S RENTED HOUSE was located on the outskirts of the city. Some people might consider the genteelly shabby neighborhood to be too plebeian for a star of Mitch's stature, but Tory knew that he'd never cared all that much for creature comforts. She'd witnessed his ability to fall asleep just as quickly on the damp ground in the middle of the rainy season as he could in some king-size hotel-room bed. Such talent was an occupational necessity. It was also one she shared.

If the outside of the small, whitewashed bungalow was without embellishment, the inside was absolutely spartan. The few pieces of furniture had been crafted from local wood, handwoven cotton rugs were scattered over the plank flooring, a brightly hued blanket had been tossed carelessly over the back of a lumpy sofa that had seen better days.

The fact that she could see no personal items anywhere in the room did not surprise Tory. Mitch had always been like a turtle, carrying his home on his back. And although she had likewise tried to pare her belongings down to absolute essentials, she remembered his teasing comments about her insistence on carrying along moisturizer and hair conditioner, even in the jungle.

"Home, sweet home," she murmured.

"It's all I need," Mitch shot back, unreasonably defensive. "After all, I didn't come to Playa de Palma to entertain."

Tory looked at him curiously. "I was simply commenting on your talent for minimalism. It was always one of the things I admired about you."

Looking for censure in her expression and finding none, Mitch relaxed slightly. "That and my devastating good looks. And rapier wit. Not to mention my brilliant intellect."

"And let's not forget your modesty."

"I didn't figure there was any harm in pointing out what a catch I was. Just in case you decide to change your mind."

"You're not that bad a catch," Tory admitted. "If a woman were trolling, which I'm not."

"So you said." He glanced around the room, as if seeing it for the first time himself. "I guess I could've done something with the place."

"Why waste time fixing up a house you'll be leaving in just a few weeks?" Tory asked, honestly curious.

"That's what I've always thought. But I figured you might see things differently."

"But why...?" Comprehension slowly dawned. "Because I'm a woman, right? And being a woman, I should be struck with a sudden urge to start sewing gingham curtains the minute I walk in the door. Or straighten the pictures on the wall. Is that what you're saying, Mitch?"

Mitch had the grace to redden at her accusatory tone. "I suppose I was thinking of something along those lines," he admitted. "Although if you'll notice, the walls are bare. And I certainly can't picture you sewing gingham."

"Well, that's a relief."

Mitch decided that if he lived to be a hundred, he would never understand women. Allie used to get upset because he never noticed when she'd purchased a new vase, a dainty lace throw pillow for the sofa, or any of the little brass knickknacks she'd enjoyed discovering in Beirut's souks. After first professing amazement at his admittedly spartan living quarters, Allie had dedicated the first year of their marriage to redoing their rented Beirut apartment into what she considered a proper home.

Tory, on the other hand, seemed irritated that he'd even suggest she might appreciate a more homey atmosphere. Deciding that this was no time to attempt to unravel the puzzle that was the feminine mind, Mitch took a bottle of brandy from a shelf and poured it into two of the chipped water glasses that had come with the house.

"I promised to warm you up," he said, handing Tory one of the glasses. "So why don't you get out of those wet clothes and into a hot tub while I go develop the photos?"

The idea sounded heavenly. It also sounded more dangerous than Tory cared to admit. "I'm not that cold anymore," she insisted. "The brandy's all I need. To prove her point she took a long swallow. The liquor burned the back of her throat, but as it hit her stomach, she could feel the warmth spreading outward. "Terrific," she said brightly.

"If you don't get out of those wet jeans, you're going to catch a cold," he said. "Which could put La Rubia right out of business."

He had a point, Tory admitted. "Since I didn't realize that I was going to be running around in the rain, I didn't bring along a second change of clothing. The only other thing I have with me is the dress I was wearing when your doctor friend arrived to take me to his clinic."

From the look of lust in the doorman's eyes as she'd left the lobby, she knew that the backless red minidress definitely lived up to La Rubia's sexy image. That being the case, she was not about to wear it in such an intimate situation.

"I can take care of that." Reaching into a duffel bag— Mitch still hadn't got around to unpacking, Tory noticed—he pulled out an oversize navy-blue sweatshirt and a pair of gray sweatpants. "These should keep you modest enough," he said, tossing them to her. "Until your jeans dry."

Tory felt as if the cold mountain rain had chilled her all the way to her bones. The idea of a long hot bath was undeniably appealing. But she'd come here to work, not loll around in Mitch's tub.

"I should help you develop those pictures," she said with a definite lack of enthusiasm. If she was to be perfectly honest, cramped darkrooms, even with their glowing red lights, had always unnerved her.

If Mitch hadn't been watching her so closely, he would have missed the faint dread come and go in her eyes. "It'll only take a few minutes," he assured her. "Go take your bath, Tory. It's right through there."

He tilted his head toward the open bedroom door. Tory followed his gaze and drew a deep breath. Unlike the spartan style of the living room, one enormous piece of furniture took up most of the space, and the bed was even larger than king-size. The fact that it was unmade didn't surprise her. After all, she knew very few men who took the time to tidy up in the morning. And besides, she remembered when she'd thought there was something undeniably sexy about the way Mitch's mussed sheets had carried the distinctively male scent of their owner.

But speaking of sexy... The outstanding feature of the oversize bed had to be its elaborately carved headboard. Tory stared in disbelief and awe at the intricate carvings.

"Are those what I think they are?"

"Depends on what you think they are. Why don't you look a little closer?" he suggested with a devilish grin.

Tory entered the bedroom, unable to take her eyes from what proved to be amazingly detailed scenes of men and women making love.

"Gracious," she said weakly. "I've never seen anything like this."

"The man who carved this wonderfully dirty headboard is a Mayan Indian, who insists that he's following in his ancestors' footprints," Mitch explained. "The scenes are supposedly copies of rare Mayan wall paintings displayed in Mexico City's museum of anthropology."

Tory tilted her head, trying for a different perspective on one particularly amorous pair. Personally she wasn't certain such a position was physically possible. But that didn't keep the slow warmth from stirring somewhere deep within her. It was only the brandy, she assured herself. She'd simply drunk it too fast. That was all it was. It was all she could allow it to be.

"I don't know how you get any sleep," she said honestly.

Mitch chuckled. "Some nights it's harder than others." He didn't add that it had been damn near impossible since those provocative posters of La Rubia had started popping up all over the city. Especially when one woman in the center of the headboard bore an unsettling resemblance to Tory.

"Well." Tory could feel heat flooding her face, but she seemed unable to move. It was as if her feet had been nailed to the wooden floor. The wood, a dark rose-red mahogany, gleamed like warm satin. Unable to resist, Tory reached out and ran her fingers over its surface. "Subject matter aside, the workmanship is absolutely remarkable."

Mitch could tell that Tory was not unaffected by the blatantly sensual scenes. That idea, coupled with the fantasy of making love to her in a myriad of wonderful ways all over that wide soft mattress, was enough to make him hard. "I know. That was one of the reasons I bought it."

That got Tory's attention. She dragged her gaze from the headboard to Mitch's face. "You bought this bed? But where will you put it?"

He shrugged. "I'm thinking of getting a small house. Probably on the northern coast of California."

"You're going to settle down?" The idea of Mitch actually settling into a quiet suburban existence was almost too depressing to consider.

"Not really," he answered quickly, as if Tory were not the only one who considered the idea of his retirement to be anathema. "I just thought that it might be nice to have a place to get away to from time to time. Someplace that was completely mine."

"Oh." Tory thought about that for a moment, deciding that it sounded rather appealing. Albeit expensive, considering how much time he'd be able to spend there. "But why California?"

Mitch shrugged. "Why not?"

Something occurred to Tory. Something that caused a small, green-eyed monster to stir inside her. "Does this sudden need for a coastal retreat have anything to do with the fact that your ex-wife just happens to live in California?"

"Of course not."

Tory bit her lip. "Are you sure?"

Viewing Tory's atypical display of vulnerability, Mitch took the fact that she was worried about any lingering feelings he might be harboring toward Alanna as a good sign. "Positive. I grew up in the Bay area, Tory. When I returned home last year after being released, I realized that if I ever did want to put down roots, northern California is as good a place as any. Better than most."

Placing his glass upon the chipped glass top of a nearby table, he cupped her shoulders with his long fingers. Unreasonably nervous, Tory took another drink of her brandy and tried to convince herself that the renewed warmth flooding through her was from the liquor and not Mitch's intimate touch.

"I wasn't lying when I said I'd fantasized about you, Victoria," Mitch said with a frown. "More times than I cared to count."

His expression was not encouraging, given the intimate topic of this conversation. "Apparently you didn't find the experience all that enjoyable," Tory ventured.

His fingers tightened, digging into her skin. Mitch couldn't decide whether to shake her or drag her down onto that ridiculously erotic bed and make mad, passionate love to her. In the end he did neither.

"It wasn't the fantasies themselves," he said. "It was the way they left me feeling."

She had to ask. "How?"

"Guilty as hell."

"But why? Sexual fantasies are a very normal part of life," she insisted, even as she wondered how in the world they'd gotten onto such a dangerous subject. It was the bed, she concluded. That damn sexy bed.

"That's just the problem. My life wasn't really very normal in those days," Mitch said grimly.

Tory touched his arm; the muscles tensed under her fingertips. "You thought about me while you were being held captive?" she asked in a shaky voice that was barely above a whisper.

The idea of Mitch thinking about her during the most volatile years of his life was both frightening and thrilling. Frightening because it meant that perhaps what they'd shared eight years ago had been more than a mere wartime flirtation. And thrilling because she'd dreamed of him during those years, more times than she could possibly count.

Mitch's handsome face was stark; remembered pain deepened the lines etched across his forehead, those bracketing his grimly set mouth, the ones surrounding his remarkably blue eyes. There was tension in every line of his body.

"I dreamed about holding you," he said. "I remembered how well you fitted into my arms...."

He drew in a deep, ragged breath, thinking back. How guilty such sensual thoughts had left him feeling! He had been married to a wonderful, loving woman. So why, although he'd certainly experienced hundreds—hell, thousands—of fantasies and dreams about his wife during those years, had his rebellious mind insisted on drifting back to Tory?

"I used to remember how everything between us was always such a close—a perfect—fit," he continued in a low, deep voice that wrapped around Tory like a cloak of ebony velvet. "As if we'd been made to bring pleasure to each other."

"Mitch—"

When she would have pulled away, Mitch's hands moved down her arms, gripping her tightly. "No," he said, his voice turning harsher, more grating than anything she'd ever heard from him. "It's time you heard me out. So you'll know the truth."

As if sensing that she was incapable of moving, he released her long enough to drag his fingers through his hair. "Although I don't know what the hell it'll prove, it's important that you understand how I felt in those days."

He'd never told anyone. Not even Allie. Especially not Allie. Of course, in those early days after his release he'd been trying to convince everyone that he'd suffered no ill effects from his time as a hostage. For some stupid reason that he could only put down to male ego, it had seemed important to behave as if five years of captivity had proven no more strenuous than a walk in the park.

He was hurting, Tory realized. More than he'd ever admit. Feeling as if her own heart were splitting into a million crystalline pieces, she lifted a trembling hand to the side of his face. "I want to know," she whispered. "I want you to share it with me, Mitch. All of it."

Ever since his return it had been Mitch's experience that most individuals, while expressing grave regret for what had happened to him six years ago, had been afraid to hear any of the details. It was preferable, safer even, to think of his ordeal in the abstract, as an unpleasant fact of modern life that they might view on the evening news.

Tory was the first person to want to know everything. He wanted to draw her close, to bury his face in the silky fragrance of her hair, to bask in the warmth of her body. He ached to kiss her full soft lips and remember another time, when life had been unbelievably sweet and filled with golden promise. Not wanting her to think he was trying to seduce her yet again, Mitch reluctantly released her and backed away from the brink.

"Later," he told her. "After I've developed the film and you've had your bath and changed into some dry clothes."

"But—"

Unable to stop himself, he ran his knuckles down her cheek, pleased by the way the soft color bloomed under his touch. "Later," he repeated quietly.

Realizing that their relationship was on the verge of being inexorably altered yet again, Tory understood that if she was going to invite Mitch to unburden himself to her, she also had to allow him to choose the time and place.

"Have I ever told you that you can be incredibly bossy?" she asked, shooting him a mock scowl.

Mitch marveled at the way she could lift him out of the doldrums. Only a moment ago he'd felt the familiar suffocating depression about to settle over him, as it had periodically since his release. But she banished it with only a few words, a playful frown and the warmth of her soft brown eyes.

"I believe you've mentioned something about it," he said. "But we all know how you're prone to exaggeration. Don't we, Scarlett?"

"Scarlett?" Tory repeated blankly. "Oh. You're still mad because the colonel obviously has a thing for Georgia peaches."

"I'm not mad. But I sure as hell wasn't thrilled by the way you had Astor practically eating out of your lily-white hand. You can get in a world of trouble playing games with a guy like that, Tory. Although your accent has improved over the years," he added as an afterthought.

The tense mood evaporated, like morning fog under a bright tropical sun. Tory smiled. "High praise indeed from a man whose Ronald Reagan impression was the hit of the press corps' Latin American Follies."

Mitch's talent for mimicry, which he used to conduct mock interviews with renowned heads of state, had earned him an exalted place among his peers. Tory remembered how his imitation of Great Britain's former prime minister had gotten back to the Iron Lady herself. Rather than being disturbed by Mitch's biting satire, the prime minster had actually written him a charming letter, inviting him to dine with her the next time he was in London.

"Ah, but the routine would have been nothing without your First Lady," Mitch insisted. "You had her down pat."

"We made a good team," she said with a soft, reminiscent smile.

Mitch ducked his head and brushed his lips lightly, unthreateningly against hers. The kiss, which ended much too soon, left her skin tingling. "In case you hadn't noticed, we still do, sweetheart."

With that he was gone, leaving her to sink onto the mattress and wonder how she was going to keep things on a professional basis, when the idea of making love with Mitchell Cantrell was becoming more seductive with each passing minute.

WHILE MITCH WORKED in the laundry room he'd turned into a darkroom, developing the film he'd taken that afternoon, he was forced to employ every ounce of willpower he possessed to keep himself from going into the bathroom and sharing Tory's hot tub. Despite her continual claim that she wanted to keep their relationship free of entanglements, her willingness to hear about his days in Lebanon proved that they were already emotionally involved. That being the case, he felt certain she would not send him away. But since he'd given his word that the next move would be hers, he had no choice but to wait for her to come to him.

Mitch could only hope it wouldn't be too long.

After developing the film, he made a contact sheet, selecting a few of the more incriminating shots for en-

largement. As he watched the images slowly appear in
the developer, Mitch knew that he and Tory had stumbled across dynamite. The trick now was to figure out
a way to use it without blowing themselves up, right
along with Astor and General Ramirez.

There was a knock on the darkroom door. "Mitch?"

"Just a sec." He hung the last shot up to dry, turned
on the overhead light and opened the door. "I don't
think the colonel's going to be submitting these to the
base newspaper."

Tory felt a surge of excitement when she viewed the
still-wet black-and-white photos. "We have him!" she
exulted. "All we have to do is hand these over to the
proper authorities in the States, and Ramirez is history."

"It's not going to be that easy."

"What do you mean?"

Before Mitch could answer, there was a sharp rap on
the front door. "Right on time," he said.

His guest, whom Mitch introduced as James Slater,
was a darkly tanned man in his late forties. His shoulders were wide, his body firm, and the eyes beneath the
iron-gray crew cut that was a twin of Colonel Astor's
were hard and unblinking. Although he was casually
dressed in khaki pants and a white cotton shirt with the
sleeves rolled up to the elbows, Tory had the immediate impression that he would have been more comfortable in a military uniform. He couldn't have stood
straighter if someone had dropped a rod of steel down
his back.

"Jim is in the import-export business," Mitch explained. "I thought he might have a line on any smug-
gled artifacts."

"Really, Mitch," Tory complained. "I thought you said we were partners."

"We are."

"Then why don't you give me some credit for a modicum of intelligence?" she countered. Folding her arms across her chest, she turned toward Slater. "CIA, right?"

Slater exchanged a brief look with Mitch, who shrugged and said, "Hell, you may as well tell her, or we'll never get any peace."

"You're close," Slater acknowledged with reluctant admiration. "Actually I'm army intelligence."

Tory nodded, satisfied. "I knew it was something like that. Are you going to begin an investigation of Colonel Astor?"

"The investigation has been ongoing for some time," Slater revealed. "What we've been waiting for is proof of collusion between Astor and Ramirez." He looked at Mitch. "As soon as you called me from the cantina about the photos, I thought we might have finally stumbled onto something useful."

"I don't know how useful they'll be," Mitch warned. "But you're welcome to check them out."

By the time Slater left an hour later, Tory was extremely frustrated. "I still think the two of you are being too cautious," she complained. "The pictures speak for themselves. The army ought to arrest Astor and his men right now."

"Even if we had proof of what's in the mailbags, which we don't, there still isn't any concrete evidence implicating Ramirez," Mitch pointed out.

"But it's his house."

"So?"

"We both know that none of his men would dare run a smuggling ring out of the general's home without his knowledge. They're too afraid of him," she insisted.

"With good reason," Mitch reminded her. "Which is why we're going to move slowly on this, Tory."

"But we don't have time!" She looked up at him, her eyes wide and distressed. "Don't you see? If Ramirez is elected in Tuesday's election, it'll be even harder for the U.S. to extradite him. We have to bring him down now. Before he can claim that he has the people of La Paz behind him."

She dragged her fingers through her chestnut hair and began to pace the room furiously. "I want to do this right, but all I can think about is Amy lying in that hospital bed, her body and her spirit broken, while Ramirez is running around free, adding millions of dollars to his various secret bank accounts." She spun around, her eyes moist with angry tears. "Dammit, Mitch," she complained, "it just isn't fair."

Mitch had already learned the hard way that life wasn't always fair. But he didn't think Tory needed to hear that little homily right now. "I know, sweetheart."

The soft, gentle tone proved to be her undoing. Tired of being strong, exhausted by holding in her anger and frustration, Tory allowed the dam to burst. "I wanted to help her." Covering her face with her hands, Tory began to weep.

Mitch put his arms around her, holding her close, the hand on her back offering comfort, not seduction. "I know."

"I wanted to make it better," she sobbed into the hard line of his shoulder. "Like I always have."

Mitch knew little of comforting women. The women of his acquaintance wore their self-reliance on their sleeves like a badge of honor. As had Tory. He'd always marveled at her bravery, her independence, and most of all at what his father would have referred to as her old-fashioned spunk. This was a side of Tory he'd never seen. A soft, vulnerable side that had him vowing that whatever it took, he'd make certain General José Enrique Ramirez got exactly what was coming to him.

"We're going to get him, Tory," Mitch said as he held her even tighter. "I promise. You have to believe that."

Lifting her head, Tory dashed at the free-falling tears with the backs of her hands. She stared at him for a minute, wondering what she'd done right in her life to have been granted a second chance with this man. "I believe in you," she managed to say.

He smiled and pressed his lips against her hair. "That's a good start."

9

WORKING TOGETHER in the compact, utilitarian kitchen, Tory and Mitch prepared a supper of salad, rice and grilled beef. Although neither of them had ever claimed to be more than an adequate cook, the simple meal turned out to be quite appetizing. Still, Tory spent most of the time pushing the food around on her plate while Mitch refrained from talking.

The tension built as they moved outside onto the brick patio that took up most of the small backyard, for their coffee. Mitch sipped at the dark brew and wished it were something stronger.

Tory sensed his discomfort and wished that she could soothe him as he had consoled her earlier. But she was intuitive enough to realize that Mitch had to exorcise whatever demons had a hold on him before he could successfully move on with his life.

"Would you like a refill?" she asked softly.

Mitch considered going for the coffee himself; he could always fortify it while he was in the kitchen. Knowing that he couldn't take a drink every time he had to think about his captivity, however, he declined. "No, thanks. I'm fine."

Are you? Tory wanted to ask. *Really?* Realizing that this was no time to push, she held her tongue.

They were sitting quietly beside one another on a wicker lounge, contemplating the stars and listening to the soft sea breeze rustle the palm fronds overhead. The night air was perfumed with the fragrance of bougainvillea and frangipani.

"I'd been in the south," he said, suddenly breaking the silence. "Sleeping on the ground, evading blockades, trying to avoid being killed in the constant cross fire."

"In other words," Tory murmured, "it was just another working day in war-torn Lebanon."

"Yeah." It helped that she understood, he decided. That she realized what he was doing there and why. Allie never had. Not that he would have expected her to. But his bride's obvious fear and dislike of his dangerous life-style had tormented Mitch during those long, lonely years in captivity.

"I wasn't due back in Beirut for another day or two, but Allie wanted to celebrate our anniversary."

"I can understand that." Tory, the reporter, understood Mitch's driving need for the story; Tory, the woman, empathized with Alanna Cantrell's desire to share her first wedding anniversary with her husband.

"So could I. I could also understand her need to overlook the blackened, charred rubble and pretend that the city was as it had been—the Paris of the Middle East."

"That must have been quite a challenge."

"An impossible one. But it was important to her, and since I felt guilty about bringing her to a place where she was obviously frightened and unhappy so much of the time, I was determined to try and make things up to her. At least for this one night."

He took a deep breath. "I had a bottle of French champagne waiting on ice in the honeymoon suite at the hotel, and since I figured she'd be homesick for San Francisco's spring flowers, I met her after work with a fistful of tulips."

Amazing! Tory reflected. Even for Mitch. "Where on earth did you find tulips in Beirut?"

"It wasn't that difficult. A friend of mine was due back from Amsterdam, where his wife had had a baby. I simply asked him to bring the tulips back with him."

"I've always admired your flair, Cantrell," Tory said.

"Thanks." His expression grew distant. "We were walking to the hotel and had stopped to buy some fruit from a pushcart vendor. To tell the truth, I wasn't thrilled about having to come back early, but when I paid the guy for those shiny red apples, I was surprised by how happy I was."

Tory bit back the feeling of jealousy his words aroused. For heaven's sake, both Mitch and Alanna Cantrell had suffered for years. Who was she to want to deny them this small pleasure?

"That must have helped," she offered quietly. "Reliving that feeling during your captivity."

"It sure as hell did. Sometimes it was the only thing that kept me sane." He sighed deeply and fell silent for a time. "It happened so fast," he said finally. "This bronze car pulled up to the curb, came to a stop with an earsplitting squeal of brakes, and three men armed with automatic rifles burst out of the car, shoved me into the back seat and tore off."

There was another little pool of silence. Tory closed her eyes and imagined the terror Alanna Cantrell must have felt.

"The first four days I spent blindfolded," he continued in a low, flat, emotionless voice. "They tied me to a straight-backed wooden chair and lashed my hands to the back legs. Then they told me that they'd kill me if I said a single word."

Something clenched Tory's heart. "Oh, Mitch," she whispered.

"After about a week, I was stuffed into the trunk of a car and moved to the basement of an apartment building in suburban Beirut. That's when things got really bad. I spent the next six months crammed into a filthy room the size of a broom closet. There wasn't any light, and I shared the floor with the rats.

"Not that I got that much sleep," he said bitterly. "Every time the guards caught me drifting off, they'd start beating and kicking me again." He dragged one hand over his face and took a deep breath. "But the worst part was the way they kept taunting me, telling me that my government, and what was even harder to listen to, my wife, had abandoned me."

"No one abandoned you, Mitch. It's just that no one knew where you were. And then, after they announced that they'd executed you and released that photo, the State Department declared you dead." Tory took a deep, shuddering breath. "That was the worst day of my life."

Her soft admission was all he needed. Mitch felt as if a door had at last been unlocked. The words came pouring out, sometimes tripping over each other as he told her about the meager diet of plain rice and tea, about his pneumonia, the torture, all the times he'd been wrapped like a mummy, crammed into car trunks and ambulances and taken away in the middle of the night, driven around the city in a purposefully convoluted manner to confuse his sense of direction.

"Once they stuffed me into a coffin," he said. "But it was too short, so they had to tie my wrists and ankles together, arching my back so they could shut it. I don't know how long I was locked in there, but after a while the whole crazy thing turned surrealistic and I couldn't decide whether I really was dead or simply imagining it."

Tears began to trail down Tory's face. She ignored them, remaining silent. Mitch talked for hours. The sky changed from ebony to deep purple, then to a soft silvery tint as the sun prepared to make its appearance. Dawn was painting the horizon with a delicate rose when Mitch's inner motor finally ran down. Somewhere in the distance a cock crowed.

He was exhausted. But there was one more thing. Massaging the back of his rigid neck with his hand, he garnered strength for one last confession. "During all those years I tried to keep from going crazy by thinking about the people I loved. I pictured my mother, waiting for me to come home. And Allie. I was determined to stay alive. For her."

The words didn't hurt nearly as much as Tory thought they might have. Once she accepted the idea that Alanna Cantrell had been what kept Mitch alive all those years, she was immensely grateful to his former wife.

"But I thought about you, too," he insisted hoarsely. "More times than I could count. And although I invariably felt almost adulterous after a particularly sensual dream or fantasy, I still couldn't get you out of my mind."

Turning toward her, he took hold of both her hands and looked into her face. "I've had a lot of time to think about that, Victoria, and I've come to the conclusion that the reason I couldn't forget you was because a very strong, elemental part of me didn't want to."

"I never forgot you, either," she whispered. Reaching up, she traced his grimly set lips with a fingernail. "In fact, I have a confession of my own."

Her light caress caused the carefully banked fires inside Mitch to begin to burn anew. He decided that if she didn't stop touching him, he wouldn't be able to keep his word.

"A confession?"

Very deliberately she brushed her lips against his. The kiss, as soft as a whisper, caused needs to thunder through him. "I lied."

He closed his eyes as she caught his earlobe between her teeth. "About what?"

Tory could hear the husky desire in his voice and laughed quietly as she nibbled on the corded muscles of his neck. "About not wanting you to make love to me."

Afraid that she was only responding to the moment, that she'd change her mind afterward, then blame him for breaking his promise, Mitch caught hold of her chin and held her gaze to his. The look he gave her was long and deep, assuring her that what was about to happen was as important to him as to her.

"Once isn't going to be enough," he warned.

"You've no idea how happy that idea makes me."

Tory began unbuttoning his shirt. Her hands grazed over the hard muscles, his ribs, her fingers played with the line of gold hair arrowing down to his waistband. She pushed the material away and pressed moist kisses against his chest. Tory could feel Mitch's heart pounding wildly beneath her lips, matching the rhythm, beat for beat, of her runaway pulse.

"You do realize that you're making me crazy." Mitch took her hand and pressed it against his lower body.

"Goodness." Tory bit her lip, trying not to grin as she looked up at him. "Did I do that?"

Mitch decided that he'd never seen anything more exciting than the devilment in her eyes. "What the hell do you think?"

"I think," she said, struggling with the cumbersome buttons on the fly of his faded jeans, "that the first thing I'm going to do when the stores open this morning is buy you a pair of pants with a zipper."

"Perhaps I can help."

He stood up, his deft fingers dispatching the row of buttons. Just the sight of him, looking rumpled and sexy, was enough to send thrills skimming beneath her skin. But when he slid first the jeans and then his white briefs over his hips and down his legs, Tory forgot her vow to take things slowly.

He was tall and lean, with the power and endurance of a long-distance runner, his deeply tanned skin smooth and tight over his bones. He was beautifully formed, possessing the type of build that ancient sculptors had once immortalized in gleaming bronze.

Mitch told himself that he should feel foolish, standing naked on display like this, but the blatant admiration in Tory's eyes made him feel more a man than he had in years.

"I'd almost convinced myself that my memory had played tricks on me," she murmured, running her hands over the width of his shoulders before going on to explore the ridged strength of his chest, his hard flat stomach.

"But you're even more magnificent than I remembered." Kneeling in front of him, Tory kneaded the corded muscles on the inside of his thighs, marveling at the tension beneath her touch. *Mine,* she thought incredulously. *He's all mine.* When her fingers curled through the crisp nest of hair at his groin, Mitch groaned aloud.

Her dark, throaty laugh, the tender touch of her hands, her breath, which was like a soft summer breeze against his heated flesh, all conspired to drive Mitch to madness. He felt control slipping away beneath her caressing fingertips; ruthlessly he forced it back. "For God's sake, Tory—"

His hands tangled in her hair. Urging her to her feet, he whipped the oversize sweatshirt over her head, giving his mouth access to her breasts. He began to suckle deeply, creating a slow, respondent pull between Tory's legs.

When his hand slid beneath the waistband of the baggy sweatpants, roving over her stomach, then lower still to cup her intimately, her entire body threatened to shatter. The earth tilted, control shifted.

"Please." Desire, need, want. Each was too weak a word to describe the glorious sensations ricocheting through her body. As his wicked fingers made exquisite contact with the soft, sensitive flesh, Tory craved more.

She pressed against his hand in a desperate plea for relief, knowing that she was revealing a helplessness she'd never shown to any man. Not even to Mitch. But even as she struggled against it, she welcomed her capitulation. Because with surrender came trust. And love.

"Please," she repeated in a ragged whisper. "Make love to me, Mitch."

Needing no second invitation, Mitch scooped her up and carried her into the bedroom. He didn't take his eyes from hers as he slid the pants down her legs, ridding her of the last barrier of material between them. Then he lowered himself slowly, looking deep into her eyes, seeing the thrill of pleasure as burning flesh met flesh.

The mattress gave as they moved over it, the sheets grew hot and tangled. But when Tory would have rushed, Mitch set the pace. His fingers were like feathery brands, inflaming her, scorching his claim on her softly yielding flesh. His questing lips and hands tempted, teased and aroused.

As Mitch explored every fragrant nook and cranny of Tory's body, he found it to be both remarkably the same, yet different. Her firm, uplifted breasts were fuller, more rounded than he remembered, but when his tongue flicked over the rosy-pink nipples, making them hot and hard, she trembled in a way that was heartbreakingly familiar.

Her waist was as slender as ever, curving outward in a subtle sweep to hips that were less angular, more womanly, than they'd been eight years ago. He pressed a trail of openmouthed kisses against her warm flesh, finding to his delight that her taste—the heady flavor of sweet, dark passion—was deliciously unchanged.

Tory felt herself melting under his caressing hands, slowly sliding into ecstasy. She heard herself sigh his name as his mouth lingered at the inside of her thighs.

The backs of her knees. Her ankles. The white-hot passion she'd felt earlier metamorphosed into a warm, golden glow that left her weak. She lay steeped in it, her limbs liquid, her skin rippling under his touch as she basked in a tenderness like nothing she'd ever known.

Her mind was clouded with a soft, sensual mist, but her body was acutely alive, guided by feeling alone. With every movement of his mouth on her flesh, her quiet sighs became moans; with every stroking touch of his hands she trembled. His morning beard was like the finest grade of sandpaper against her heated flesh, stimulating already sensitized nerves. Needs poured forth from every pore. And still he refused to rush.

Through the shimmering clouds of pleasure, Tory realized that Mitch was blocking his own wants so that she might experience bliss. That knowledge gave rise to something infinitely more thrilling, more scintillating than passion.

She flowed against him, no longer pliant. Her hands stroked his back and tempted. Her lips skimmed over his hot damp flesh and tormented. Her mouth found his and clung greedily.

Mitch was poised over her, every muscle taut, gleaming with passion. "I need you, Tory." The words were wrenched from him, hoarse and urgent. Ageless passions churned in his storm-blue eyes. "More than I ever could have imagined."

"Oh, Mitch." All the emotions Tory was feeling shimmered in his whispered name. "I need you, too. So much." She dug her nails into his shoulders, pulling him down and into her. She opened for him, gasping her pleasure as they merged, body to body, heart to heart.

He filled her to a desperate point beyond delirium. Harder and faster he took her, driving her, driving himself, to a crest that was impossibly, dangerously high. Then higher still, from that summit to an even steeper one. Breathless, Tory clung to him as they raced into the mists.

When she opened her eyes with a soft cry of excitement, Mitch saw the astonished pleasure shining in those warm, doe-brown depths and vowed to remember her this way always. Then, giving in at last to the demands of his own body, he closed his mouth upon hers and followed Tory over the edge.

TORY WOKE with a slow, languid stretch and realized that they'd slept for some time. The sun was higher in the sky, fast burning off the early-morning fog with its bright yellow Caribbean light. Her body felt unusually heavy; glancing down she saw Mitch, his arms and legs sprawled over her, as if to prevent her from slipping away while he dozed.

Not that he'd have to use force to keep her in his bed, Tory thought to herself with a wry smile. Because last night had proven that whatever else might have changed between them, things like desire and passion had remained exactly the same.

Giving in to impulse, Tory played with the golden ends of his hair, remembering what he'd told her, right before he'd driven them both into oblivion. He needed her. Steeped in the dark passion of the night, she'd taken his words to be a commitment. A promise of the future that they had once foolishly allowed to slip out of their hands. But now, thinking about it in the cold light of day, Tory realized that there were two other possible explanations.

The first was that perhaps he'd made love to her in a desperate attempt to recapture the past. To return to a time when life had been simpler, when his dreams, both waking and sleeping, had not been filled with terror.

Depressing though that possibility was, the alternative was even worse. Perhaps, after having finally revealed the details of his torturous five years in captivity, making love to Tory had merely been a means of catharsis. A putting away of the past, so he could move on to the future. A life—she had to force herself to think this—that might not include her. The idea hurt, like the low, dull ache of a tooth that had been neglected for too long.

Uttering a soft sigh, Tory decided to put the question away for now. She'd analyze what was happening between Mitch and herself later, when she could think straight, free of the conflicting emotions that kept tumbling around in her head. Closing her eyes, she drifted back to sleep.

IT WAS THE PHONE that woke her, jarring her from a pleasantly erotic dream. Sitting up, Tory struggled to return to reality as she listened to Mitch's murmur in the other room.

A moment later he appeared in the open doorway, dressed in jeans and a faded blue chambray shirt. "That was Dr. Mendoza," he informed her. "The hotel manager just called his clinic, asking if you were well enough to perform tonight."

The last lingering vestiges of her sensual dream were wiped away by his matter-of-fact tone. "Good morning to you, too."

Mitch sauntered lazily into the room and sat down on the edge of the bed. He wrapped a thick swath of her hair around his hand, enjoying its texture, remembering how it had felt, draped lushly over his body like strands of molten silk. His finger traced the outline of her ear. "Do you have any idea how sexy you look in the morning, all warm and flushed from making love?"

How was it that such a simple touch could send such excitement through her? Already afraid of losing him, Tory concentrated on keeping her voice steady. "So what did you tell the doctor?"

He felt her tense, but deciding not to comment on it, Mitch continued to stroke her hair. "I assured him that we'd have you safely back at the clinic within the hour."

"That's not much time." She couldn't quite hide her disappointment that he was so willing to let her go. After all they'd shared.

"No." He took her hand and pressed his lips to her palm. "All the more reason not to waste any of it."

When had she become such a coward? Tory asked herself. How could she possibly be afraid of the fragile touch of lips against skin? A myriad of warnings raced through her mind, but she ignored them. Lifting her face for his kiss, she allowed herself to risk.

10

"I THINK I made a big mistake," Mitch said. He was leaning against the bathroom doorjamb, watching Tory create La Rubia before his eyes.

"Mitch Cantrell, hotshot foreign correspondent, actually admitting he made a mistake?" Tory asked absently. "That's enough to renew my faith in miracles." She scowled as she brushed the powder blush onto her cheek, trying to keep from looking like a clown.

Mitch ignored her sarcasm. "Instead of having Mendoza tell the hotel manager that you're better, I should have had him prescribe bed rest."

Tory met his laughing eyes in the mirror. "I would have liked that."

"You've no idea how glad I am to hear it." Coming up behind her, he took hold of her shoulders and gently turned her around. "I thought you might wake up with regrets." He smoothed the rosy blush up the slanting line of her cheekbone with his thumb, blending the cosmetic color with the natural warmth that bloomed beneath his stroking touch.

Tenderness flowed from him into her. Tory felt it and fought it. "I did." Unwilling to meet his probing look, she went into the other room, where La Rubia's golden tresses were hidden away in her overnight bag.

"But you're still here," Mitch said when she returned.

"I've already told you, I intend to bring down Ramirez." Tugging on the wig, she began to shove the telltale chestnut strands out of sight. "You promised to help me. It's as simple as that."

Simple, hell. Nothing about Tory Martin had ever been simple. So why should this be any different? "So that's all I am?" His voice was deceptively calm. "A means to an end?"

"You know that what we did...what we experienced..." She faltered under the intense gaze that his colleagues had always referred to as his *60-Minutes* look. Taking a deep breath, Tory tried again. "You were wonderful, Mitch. We were wonderful together. We always were."

"I see." Mitch folded his arms over his chest. "So you're also hanging around because of great sex."

She wished he wouldn't put it that way. "You don't have to make it sound so cheap."

And she didn't have to make it sound so insignificant, Mitch considered darkly. "Sorry," he said. "I guess I've lost my knack for soft words. Six years without a woman tend to make a guy lose some of his polish."

"Six years?" Tory stared at him as she digested that. "I thought...well, after all, you have been free for a year, and you always had such a strong...I mean, I know how you always enjoyed... Six years," she repeated on a note of disbelief.

"Despite what I assume you were going to refer to as my strong sex drive, when I was first released, I spent some time in the hospital. Then, once I got home things were...difficult."

Mitch sighed. "At first I thought that it would just take time, that Alanna needed to get used to the idea of her husband returning from the grave, so to speak. Later I discovered that the distance between us was caused by the fact that she'd fallen in love with another man."

"That must have been difficult." Other man or not, Tory decided that Alanna Cantrell must have held the world's record for self-restraint if she'd been able to avoid falling under Mitch's seductive spell.

"It sure as hell wasn't easy," Mitch said. "Looking back on it, I think we both realized early on in our marriage that we were hopelessly mismatched. But I'd wanted her, and—"

"What Mitchell Cantrell wants, he gets," Tory filled in.

"Not always," he reminded her dryly. "Anyway, after I came down here, the months passed and I drifted into a fairly comfortable celibacy. And although I received some offers, I really didn't want a woman," he told her. "Until you."

When Tory would have looked away, his hand cupped her chin. "Do you have any idea how much I've thought about you since those damn posters started springing up all over town?"

"No."

"Too much." He swore. "Too damn much."

"Am I suppose to apologize?"

His fingers tightened. Something flashed in his eyes, anger or desire, Tory couldn't tell which. "We've just been about as intimate as two people can be, Victoria," he said. "I'd say that entitles me to at least a modicum of honesty."

Her throat was dry. Tory swallowed. "I haven't lied to you, Mitch." His arched brow was argument enough.

"All right," she admitted, "perhaps I wasn't exactly truthful about my reasons for being in La Paz. But I could never lie to you in bed." No. Bed was one place where Tory had always been ruthlessly honest. No one could fake such unbridled passion, not even as accomplished an actress as she had proven to be.

"One question."

Not willing to trust her voice, Tory nodded.

"If I'd asked you to marry me back then, what would you have said?"

She couldn't think. Why was he the only man who'd ever made her fumble for words? Tory knew the answer only too well. Hadn't she asked herself that question a thousand—a million—times? But if she told Mitch the truth, the last of her defenses would be stripped away. Instead she gave him the only answer that wouldn't make them both regret what might have been.

"I would have said no." She forced a calm smile and wondered how long it would take for the ache to pass. "What we had was wonderful, Mitch. More than wonderful. But it never would have survived in the real world."

Mitch tried to accept the answer for what it was. Hadn't he told himself that very same thing eight years ago as he'd packed for Beirut? "I suppose not," he murmured. He dropped his hand to his side. "You'd better finish getting ready. The hotel's sending a limo to the clinic to pick you up." Turning on his heel, he left the room. A moment later, Tory heard the front door open and close.

She picked up the crimson lip pencil, only to put it back down again when she realized that her hand was trembling. Frustrated, she threw it into her bag and went outside, where Mitch was waiting in the Jeep.

They didn't speak until they were almost at the clinic. Mitch's stony profile could have been carved on Mount Rushmore, and his hands gripped the steering wheel in a cold, angry way that made her wonder if he was fantasizing about putting them around her throat.

"Will I see you later?" she asked.

He didn't take his eyes from the crowded street. "I've got something to take care of, but I should have things wrapped up in time to catch your first show."

"What are you going to do? Does it have something to do with Ramirez?"

"Indirectly."

Excitement flared. "I don't have anything to do until this evening. Let me come with you."

"Sorry, but it'd be better for everyone concerned if you stayed out of trouble for the remainder of the day."

"Dammit, Mitch!"

He shot her an amused, sideways glance. "That's a relief."

"What?" Hating the way his dark eyes were laughing at her, Tory conveniently forgot that only minutes earlier she would have given anything for one of his devastating smiles.

"I thought you might be planning to sulk all day."

"I wasn't the one sulking. You were."

"Me?" The laughter faded, replaced by sheer incredulity. "I never sulk."

"Of course you do," Tory returned. "Whenever you don't get your own way."

"Your imagination, lady, is not to be believed."

"You just won't admit that you're capable of acting like a five-year-old," she countered.

When he stopped at a red light, they exchanged a long, challenging look. Mitch was the first to speak. "Some things never change."

"Neither do some people," she said pointedly.

He surprised her by laughing. "Do you know that I can't remember the last time I felt so frustrated. Or so good?"

It was Tory's turn to smile. "Perhaps it's the company."

His gaze grew thoughtful. "Perhaps it is."

Behind them the blare of horns alerted them to the fact that light had turned to green. Shifting into gear, Mitch drove through the intersection.

Tory spent the remainder of the brief drive to the clinic trying to convince Mitch to let her in on whatever he was doing. She threatened, cajoled, yelled and pouted. She did everything short of pulling out the crocodile tears, which she reluctantly decided was overacting, even for her.

"I didn't like the way Astor looked at us," Mitch said.

"What way was that?"

"As if he smelled a rat."

"Nonsense. He believed every honey-coated word." Tory grinned. "In case y'all have forgotten, sugah, Ah just happen to be a dynamite actress," she drawled.

Mitch would have liked to believe her. He would have felt vastly relieved if he could only convince himself that Astor had been so easy to fool. But as he pulled up behind Dr. Mendoza's Calle del Progreso clinic, Mitch found himself unable to relax.

The timing was dangerously close. Tory had no sooner slipped through the back door of the clinic when the limousine dispatched by the hotel manager glided up to the front of the modest stone building. When she arrived back at the Hotel de la Revolución, the manager was on hand to greet her. He asked about her health, his dark eyes revealing concern.

"I'm feeling much better," she assured him in the fluent, melodic tones of Latin American Spanish. "But I believe I'll go upstairs and take a long nap. I'm still a bit tired."

As she entered the suite, Tory realized she'd spoken the truth. Exhaustion suddenly came crashing down upon her. Slipping out of the red mini dress, Tory pulled off La Rubia's artfully tousled blond hair, tossed the wig onto a nearby chair and sank gratefully onto the bed.

She was still sleeping when Mitch arrived early that evening. Pulling up a chair beside the bed, he sat quietly as sunshine gave way to the soft blue shadows of dusk.

She was clad only in a pair of silk panties the pale color of sea mist, and a matching lace bra, and although he knew he could be accused of voyeurism, Mitch couldn't deny that he was enjoying the opportunity to watch her undetected. She was as beautiful as ever. Just as desirable. And, he reminded himself with a faint smile, as frustrating. There were times when he wanted to wring her lissome neck. But then there were those other instances, when he longed to bury himself in her softness and never let go.

How much had changed in three short days! How much *he* had changed! Before Tory's arrival in La Paz he'd been drifting, oddly dissatisfied with his work and his life, but not knowing what to do about it. Then, after making love with her, as he drifted comfortably from passion to languor and into sleep, a tantalizing thought had flickered in the far reaches of his mind.

He'd even been foolishly tempted to mention it to her. But then she'd insisted that what they'd shared had been merely a fling. A quenching of shared mutual desires. Nothing more.

Giving up on solving the dilemma for now, Mitch decided that Tory had been sleeping long enough. After all, it had been hours since he'd kissed her. Made love to her.

"Tory. Sweetheart."

Tory murmured in sleepy delight as he nuzzled her neck.

She was warm and pliant; Mitch found waking her more pleasurable than he could have imagined. "Rise and shine."

"Mmm." She stretched deliciously under the caressing touch of his hand.

Lying down beside her, he propped himself on one elbow and trailed lazy fingers down her throat, across her shoulders, over the soft peaks of her lace-covered breasts. "You've got a show in a few hours." Fascinated by the pebbling of her nipples, he took them between his fingers and tugged lightly. "And you can't do it from bed."

Had she ever felt such contentment? Tory wondered as she cuddled against him. Such pleasure? Never. Not even when they'd been together eight years ago. In those days Mitch had been the teacher, she the eager student. Both in the field and in bed. During the day he'd taught her how to track down leads, interview reluctant sources, survive under circumstances that would have made the average reporter turn tail and run back to some nice, safe suburban daily. At night, alone in the moon-spangled darkness, he'd taught her to understand passion.

She opened one eye. "How can you be here and in my dream at the same time?" she asked drowsily.

"You were dreaming of me?" Male pride soared. "Was it a good dream?"

Tory flushed at the erotic memory. "I suppose it was pretty good. As dreams go." A soft smile curled her lips. "Don't let it go to your head."

"Me? Never." Mitch brushed a tousled curl from her cheek. "So what were we doing in this pretty good dream?"

With a little laugh, she twined her arms around his neck. "Let me show you."

THEY HAD JUST FINISHED a dinner of spicy, West Indian soup, grilled lobster in a citrus mousseline and fresh herb bread when Mitch leaned back in his chair and silently observed Tory.

After what seemed an eternity she finally asked, "What's wrong?"

"Why should anything be wrong?"

"You keep staring at me."

"I'm not staring. I'm looking. Do you know what I've discovered?"

"What?"

"That looking at you is becoming one of my favorite things to do." His eyes gleamed with masculine appreciation. "You really are extraordinarily lovely."

"And you still haven't lost your silver tongue," she said.

Mitch's shoulders lifted in a slight shrug. "It's the truth. And as much as I'd love to take you back to bed and point out all my favorite spots on your delectable body, I do have a piece of news to impart."

"Oh? About Ramirez?"

"In a way. One of the detectives on the Playa de Palma police force located the car that struck your sister."

Tory found the news as unbelievable as it was exciting. "But how? After all, everyone knows that the police are nothing but Ramirez's puppets."

"Believe it or not, there are a few honest officers silently struggling against the politicization of the police force," Mitch assured her. "In case you're interested, the car was hidden in a garage in one of the barrios."

"Do they know who it belongs to?"

"Yes. But unfortunately, it was reported stolen the morning of your sister's accident."

"It was not an accident," Tory pointed out firmly. "And if the car was stolen, then we've run into another dead end."

Mitch leaned forward, reaching across the small table to smooth away the frown lines that had formed on her forehead. "Not necessarily. My informant tells me that they've located a person who says he knows who was driving the car that night. If this tipster's lead turns out to be on the level, it should only be a matter of time before they've apprehended the guy."

Tory wanted to believe. But experience had taught her that nothing was as it seemed in this country. "If

Ramirez is involved, why would anyone risk his life to help the police?"

Mitch reminded himself that he was dealing with a crackerjack reporter—a woman who never took things at face value. One more thing they had in common, he reflected. If he were inclined to keep score. "Perhaps he considers himself a good citizen."

"Sure," Tory countered. "And if you look outside, you'll see pigs flying all over the beach."

"You're a cynic, Victoria Martin."

"I'm a realist."

"Perhaps the reward had something to do with it."

"The reward? I didn't offer any reward." Actually she'd wanted to, but Amy's hospital bills—along with La Rubia's extensive, but necessary wardrobe—had eaten up every cent of her small savings account and were rapidly devouring her Associated Press salary as well.

"I did."

Tory stared at him. "You? Why?"

"Because she's your sister. You care about her. And I care about you," he said simply.

Tory felt the traitorous moisture springing up behind her lids and resolutely blinked it away. "I'm going to pay you back."

He knew better than to refuse. "Fine."

"How much did you offer?"

When he casually tossed off a sum that was equal to three months' pay, Tory stared. "So much?"

"You get what you pay for, Tory. I thought I'd taught you that."

She dragged her hands through her hair. "I know, but . . ." She forced herself to meet his tender gaze. "It's going to take me a while to come up with that much money."

"You can take as much time as you want," Mitch assured her. "I certainly don't need it. Everything I own can fit into two duffel bags, and my network salary more than pays for my needs. Not to mention a horribly embarrassing sum I received for the book."

He looked so uncomfortable, Tory couldn't help smiling. "Poor Mitch. It must be terrible to be rich."

"I suppose it beats being poor," he acknowledged reluctantly. "But you know that money and possessions never meant anything to me."

"I know." It had always been one of the things she'd liked about him. When she'd first met the famous television star, she'd expected him to be insufferable, filled with himself. But except for an understandable pride in his work—a pride that often accounted for the mostly true stories about his impatience, demanding behavior and flash-fire temper—Mitch had always been one of the nicest, gentlest men she'd ever met.

"Tell me something," she demanded. "Even if they catch the driver, why would he admit he was paid to run Amy down?" She stood up and began pacing the small balcony. "I doubt if even you have enough money to make him testify against Ramirez."

"You never know. A lot depends on Tuesday's election. If Ramirez wins, as he's expected to, the man will probably plead guilty to reckless driving and go to jail without implicating the general. On the other hand, if Ramirez loses . . ."

Tory turned around and looked at him incredulously. What did he know? "Is that possible?"

"Anything's possible," Mitch said with a curious smile that had Tory suspecting he knew a great deal more than he was telling.

So what else was new?

"ARE YOU SURE I sounded all right?" Tory asked later. "My throat felt a little scratchy on that last encore."

After finishing her last set she'd returned to the suite, where she and Mitch had made long, leisurely love in the oversize bathtub. Now they were sitting together, enjoying the golden glow of a passion that seemed to burn brighter and hotter each time they were together.

"You sounded terrific." Mitch scooped a handful of fragrant bubbles and spread them over her breasts. "You also looked terrific. Did I tell you that I love that black dress?" The off-the-shoulder gown had made her skin gleam like porcelain. It had also clung to her body like a lover's caress.

"You could have fooled me, the way you were in such a hurry to get it off me," she reprimanded him prettily.

He played with the bubbles, brushing a few aside to allow her rosy nipples to peek from the white foam. When he felt himself growing hard at the seductive sight, Mitch decided that his body was definitely making up for lost time.

"I didn't hear you complaining," he said.

The smile Tory gave him was as warm and loving as any a woman ever shared with her man. "And you won't," she promised softly.

Basking in the warmth of his sensual look, Tory admitted to herself that she was falling in love with Mitch all over again. More accurately, she'd never fallen out of love with him. What was she going to do when the election was over? How could she say goodbye?

"Have you decided what you're going to do after the election?" she asked softly.

Mitch frowned at the abrupt change of subject. He didn't want to talk about work. Not tonight. "I don't know. My plans and the network's plans aren't exactly in sync these days."

She would have had to be deaf to miss the aggravation in his voice. "I know the feeling." How many times had she pitched a story idea only to have her editor or bureau chief turn it down? Too many times to count. Surprisingly, it never got any easier; Tory found herself resenting the constraints put on her these days every bit as much as she had in the beginning.

"But so long as they're writing the checks, I suppose they get to call the tune," she said reluctantly.

"Actually I've been thinking of giving them back their money," Mitch divulged.

Tory stared at him. "You can't be serious."

"I've never been more serious in my life," Mitch insisted. "My contract comes up for renewal the end of this month and I'm considering not signing."

"But what will you do?"

"I don't know. Something's bound to come up." He'd talked about work enough. Taking her hand, he put it under the bubbles. "And speaking of coming up . . ."

BLISS. It was the only word to describe what Tory was feeling as she and Mitch spent the next two days exploring the country. And each other. Mitch had assured her that since he had informants combing the landscape for the driver of the car that had struck her sister, the only thing they could do was wait.

General Ramirez was still away from the city, engaged in some last-minute campaigning. Tory's only contact with the man had been a note insisting that she allow him to escort her to the ambassador's reception. She and Mitch argued about the general's invitation, Mitch insisting that the man was dangerous, Tory countering that since that was the case, she didn't dare anger Ramirez by refusing his invitation. And when the general began to encounter antigovernment demonstrators in several central valley towns, Tory suspected James Slater of covert activity.

Whatever the reason for the general's extended absence, Tory was more than a little grateful. This wonderful time apart with Mitch was something she knew she would remember for the rest of her life. They were creating memories together. Memories that would keep her warm during the long, lonely nights in the future. When she returned to her life. And Mitch resumed his own gypsy existence.

She continued performing in the lounge, but now when she sang the evocatively beautiful romantic ballads, she knew she was singing them to one man. And although she continued to be bothered by an increasingly annoying tickling sensation in the back of her throat, Mitch assured her that hers was the best female blues voice since Sarah Vaughan. An exaggeration, to be sure, but one that pleased Tory.

Through its many changes in government, La Paz had remained an extremely Catholic country. Since the hotel lounge was closed on Sundays, Tory found herself with a rare evening off. She and Mitch were taking a leisurely drive along the coast when he surprised her by turning down a narrow unpaved road that wove through fields of bright flowers.

"Where are we going?"

"It's a surprise."

"Is it about Amy?"

"No." Mitch reached out and took her hand, lacing their fingers together. "Today—and tonight—is just for us, Tory. No work, no elections, no worrying about what Ramirez is up to and how we can catch him doing it. Years from now, when we're sitting in a retirement home for aged foreign correspondents, I want to be able to think back on this weekend and remember that I'd never been happier."

Heaven help her, that was what she wanted, too. She'd come to La Paz with one thing on her mind. Revenge. But somehow when she wasn't looking, love had slipped into her heart, leaving room for little else.

Tory gasped with delight as Mitch rounded a bend and stopped the car at the edge of a secluded lagoon set against a backdrop of an exotic, emerald rain forest. The sunlit water was an endless blend of every shade of blue imaginable, rimmed by a powdery, sugar-white beach. Between the beach and the rain forest, set amid a dazzling display of tropical flowers, was a gleaming white provincial-style villa with a red-tiled roof.

"It's breathtaking," she whispered.

Mitch smiled, pleased that she was pleased. "And private," he added. "It's another world away from telephones and Slater and artifact smugglers, despots and crooked politicians."

"But if it's private—"

"Don't worry, we have permission," Mitch assured her quickly. "It's owned by one of my contacts, a highly placed official in the Ramirez government."

"You have contacts inside the government?" Tory asked, knowing even as she spoke that he would.

"Sure. How do you think I got the general's bank records? Raphael Madrid is the former head of the Bank of La Paz. He's currently serving as Ramirez's finance minister."

"That's a nice, cushy job. I guess we know who he's going to vote for."

"Actually he confessed to me just last week—off the record, of course—that he'd like to see Elena Castillo win the election."

Tory looked at him in surprise. "Latin American politics have always fascinated me," she murmured. "Nothing is ever exactly what it seems."

"You can say that again." Mitch looked at her and his expression grew both serious and tender. "But enough shoptalk." He lifted her hand to his lips. When he kissed the sensitive center of her palm, Tory felt as if she were dissolving from the knees down. "Since the election is the day after tomorrow, by tomorrow night's reception at the embassy things should really be heating up. But until then I want to pretend that you and I are the only two people in the world."

He'd certainly brought them to the right place for that, Tory decided, dragging her gaze away from Mitch's face to the shimmering expanse of blue sea. "Just like Adam and Eve," she said softly, moving into his arms. "In paradise."

11

PARADISE didn't begin to describe it. Tory couldn't recall when she'd experienced such an idyllic day. She and Mitch swam in the warm blue lagoon, explored the offshore coral reef, moving through the underwater world with a school of angelfish. They strolled along the water's edge, picking up the pink shells that had been scattered over the sand, and basked in the tropical sun, listening to the sea caressing the shore. After a light dinner they retired to one of the guest bedrooms of the villa, where they made love again and again.

It was, Tory concluded the following morning as they shared a late breakfast prepared by the villa's cook, a time tailor-made for lovers. If only she could stop sneezing.

"I wish we didn't ever have to go back," she said and sighed. They were sitting in a white lattice-framed gazebo, surrounded by brilliant blossoms that appeared to have fallen from a rainbow. Although the blazing sun was high in the sky, the air was cooled by the soft, ever-present trade winds.

Mitch reached across the table and took her hand. "Amen to that. Of course I've always enjoyed our beach excursions."

Tory laughed, recalling the long-ago day at the beach on the Pacific side of the country. The waves had pounded against the rocks and the tide had come in so high that they'd almost gotten trapped in the cove where they'd been having a picnic.

"I thought we were going to drown," she admitted.

"Never happen. I'm too tough and too stubborn to die."

Tory thought about that for a moment, knowing it was just such an attitude that allowed Mitch to keep taking chances, even after he'd discovered how dangerous those risks could be.

"I know we agreed not to talk shop," she said softly. "But I couldn't resist calling Amy."

"You called your sister? When?"

Tory suffered another bout of sneezing; Mitch handed her a tissue from the flowered cardboard box he'd brought to the gazebo from the bedroom. "Thanks. It must be all these flowers," she managed between sneezes. "I called yesterday. When you were in the kitchen planning lunch with the cook. I hope you don't mind."

"Of course not. I just couldn't figure out when we were apart long enough for you to call without me knowing it."

"Do you realize that we've been together for two days? And we haven't had a single argument?" she asked wonderingly.

"I know," Mitch said. "It must be a record."

"Or a miracle."

He smiled. "Perhaps. Lord knows we could use one about now." The smile faded as he thought of the upcoming election. They were running out of time. "So how is Amy?"

"Well enough to have fallen in love with her doctor."

"That's probably not unusual," he ventured, recalling a time several years ago in Beijing. Undergoing an emergency appendectomy, he'd opened his eyes after the operation, viewed the lovely Chinese nurse hovering over his bed like a ministering angel and fallen a little in love himself.

"I suppose not," Tory agreed. "But what is a pleasant change is that he's young, single, and appears to be just as enthralled with Amy as she is with him. She told me that he'd arranged for her to enroll in classes being offered on the local television station from the University of Miami."

"Good idea," Mitch commented with a nod. "That way, even if this romance doesn't work out, she'll have something to keep her occupied during her recovery."

"The same thought occurred to me," Tory said.

Silence settled over the table. The only sound was the occasional call of an exotic bird from the rain forest.

"I've had some news from home as well," he told her finally.

"Oh?" Tory asked on a sniffle. "When?"

"Yesterday morning, right before we left."

They'd stopped by his house so he could check his messages and pick up his mail. Tory remembered him scanning the pages of one particular letter; although the feminine handwriting on the envelope had definitely piqued her curiosity, she'd managed with a Herculean effort not to question him.

"I received a letter from my mother."

"I hope she's all right."

"Oh, she's fine. She thought I should know that Alanna gave birth to twins. A boy and a girl."

"Does that bother you?" Tory asked carefully, half dreading his answer.

"Initially I felt a little envious of Jonas Harte. But I'm not really father material. Not yet, at any rate. Perhaps in a few years. After I settle down."

Despite the seriousness of the subject, Tory couldn't resist a slight smile. "After all the stories have been covered?"

"You know me too well," he accused her with a faint smile. "So what about you? Have you ever considered having kids?"

They'd discussed the subject of children before. That night in the cave. But only because Mitch had wanted to make certain that Tory was protected from pregnancy.

"I've thought about it lately," Tory admitted. "Most women, no matter how liberated, probably can't help but consider the idea of motherhood."

Mitch felt as if he were walking on eggshells. He'd already been married to one woman who'd needed roots and a family. And although part of him truly wanted a home, a wife and children, another stronger part still needed to see what was around the next bend.

"What conclusion did you come to?" he asked with a feigned calm.

"About the same as yours. Perhaps later. Once I get this crazy need to chase down news, wherever it's breaking, out of my system. It's like an addiction, isn't it? The way it steamrollers over all your other needs."

"Exactly." He lifted a hand to her cheek. "But lately I've discovered an even stronger addiction."

His mouth touched hers, and Tory knew precisely what he meant.

LATER THAT EVENING Tory was back at the hotel, preparing for the ambassador's reception, when Mitch arrived at her suite. Her smile of greeting faded as she viewed his dark scowl.

"What's the matter?"

"Where did you get that dress?"

"This?" She turned. "I bought it in Miami."

"Where's the rest of it?"

"Don't you like it?"

The sparkling, strapless lamé flowed over her body like molten gold, clinging to every curve. Her breasts rose enticingly above the tight bodice and Mitch could have sworn that she'd dusted the silky flesh with gilt powder. As she twirled, he realized that the back of the dress was practically nonexistent, plunging precariously below the waist. Although the skirt fell to the floor, the sides were slit high on both thighs, revealing long legs clad in metallic gold stockings.

"If you sneeze tonight, you're going to provide one helluva show," he grumbled.

"Don't worry, I called down to the desk and had the concierge send up some antihistamine."

She hadn't yet inserted the contacts and her eyes, when she smiled up at him, gleamed like topaz. Although he still didn't like the idea of any other man seeing her looking so sexy, Mitch discovered that staying irritated with Tory was an impossibility.

"I brought you a present." He pulled a sheaf of papers from his jacket pocket and handed it to her.

Tory sat down on the sofa and read through the papers. When she crossed her legs, revealing a staggering amount of thigh, desire slammed into him. Mitch forced it down. For now.

"Are these what I think they are?"

"They detail Astor's smuggling transactions for the past year." Mitch managed with an effort to drag his eyes from her legs. "And surprise, surprise, the dates and figures Astor paid out for his plundered loot just happen to match the dates of deposits in the general's bank account."

"Where on earth did you get such confidential information?"

Mitch looked decidedly uncomfortable. "The important thing is that we have them."

"But Mitch—"

She had that look again. That damn terrier-with-the-bone look. "Okay, Slater and I paid a visit to the art dealer a little while ago."

"And he just gave you these? Why?"

"Perhaps it was because we said please." He sat down beside her and stroked her hair in an attempt to deter her from continuing this line of questioning.

"Somehow I strongly doubt that." When she slowly began to fall under his seductive spell, Tory caught hold of his caressing hand. "Mitch!" Her eyes widened as she viewed the bruised and scraped knuckles. "You've been in a fight!"

He grimaced. "I should have known better than to try to keep anything from Lois Lane."

"You could have been hurt."

"You should see the other guy."

"I don't believe this. You and your shadowy henchman didn't actually kill that dealer, did you?"

"Tory, Tory," Mitch complained. "Would I do that?"

"You probably wouldn't. But I wouldn't make book on Slater. Those army intelligence guys are weird."

"You don't have to worry. The dealer is, as we speak, in protective custody."

Tory's doubts about Mitch's questionable methods gave way to enthusiasm as she reread the papers she was holding in her hand. "Do you realize," she said excitedly, "that when this hits the newspaper, Ramirez is certain to lose the election!"

"It sure wouldn't help his campaign," Mitch agreed. "But it's a moot point."

"What do you mean?"

"I already took this information to Elena Castillo."

"Who was undoubtedly ecstatic."

"Not exactly. In fact, she asked me to withhold the story until after tomorrow's election."

"What?" Tory's eyes widened in disbelief. "Why on earth would she want you to do that?" She waved the papers at him. "These could cinch her victory."

"She knows that. The lady is also convinced that she can win without the scandal this story would create."

"Pollyanna lives," Tory muttered.

"She's assured me that after the election, her newly formed government will launch an investigation."

"Her newly formed government," Tory repeated scathingly. "Doesn't she understand that she's taking a terrible risk? What makes her think she can win?"

"Beats me," he said. "But she sure as hell seemed optimistic. She also added that it's important that everyone—including herself—knows that she won the hearts and minds of the people of La Paz on the issues alone."

"So," Tory mused, "as soon as the election is over, no matter who wins, you're going to break the news?"

"No."

"What?" This was getting worse by the minute.

Mitch flashed her his patented grin. "You're going to break it." He ran his bruised knuckles up her cheek. "It's your story, sweetheart. I just did some of the legwork."

"Oh, Mitch." Only a reporter as driven and committed as herself could understand exactly how generous a gift he'd made her. Whatever the outcome of the election, the story would win instant headlines all over the world. Headlines that could earn Mitch even more fame. And fortune. "I don't know how to thank you."

Mitch watched the surprised pleasure in her eyes and decided that she'd never appealed to him more than she did at this moment. Love came, instantaneous and so sharp as to be almost painful. But at the same time it felt incredibly right.

He gathered her into his arms. "Actually, now that you've brought it up, I can think of several ways."

His mouth touched hers. Softly at first, a mere whisper, more promise than proper kiss. Then a second time, lingering longer, causing her blood to heat. The third time, the urgency came crashing down upon them, creating a hunger that left her breathless, a thirst that made her weak.

Her mind and her body were locked in a spiraling onslaught of sensations. Her heart was pounding fast and furious, her head spun. When his mouth trailed down her throat her skin felt gloriously, achingly alive. When he retraced that scintillating journey to slip his tongue between her softly parted lips, Tory uttered a low sound of pleasure.

Bells were ringing, Tory realized and wrapped her arms around him, holding him close. Amazing. She'd always thought that only happened in the movies. Or romantic novels. As she pressed herself even closer to Mitch, he cursed.

"Damn phone," he muttered.

Still dazed, Tory dragged her glance to the ivory desk phone. "I suppose I'd better answer it."

"I suppose so." The reluctance in his tone matched her own.

Making her way to the desk on unsteady legs, Tory picked up the receiver. "Hello?" She put her hand over the mouthpiece. "It's the manager," she informed Mitch before returning her attention to the telephone. "Oh? Well, thank you for calling."

She put down the phone. "The general's on his way up."

Mitch dragged his hand through his hair. "Damn. Slater promised to keep him out of town for another twelve hours."

"Well, obviously something went wrong with Slater's plan," she said, disappearing into the bathroom, where her contacts were soaking in their plastic container. "And since Ramirez is on his way up here to escort me to the ambassador's reception, you'd better leave."

"I don't like the idea of leaving you alone with that guy. Especially in that dress," he said, his frown growing even darker when Tory returned to the living room, her blond wig in place, her eyes gleaming a seductive emerald green. One look at her in that dress and Ramirez could easily decide to skip the reception entirely.

"I'll be fine," Tory assured him. "All I have to do is smile a little and sing a couple of songs, then I can come back to the hotel and write my story."

"Dammit, Tory—"

Tory heard the unmistakable whirring of the elevator on the way to her floor. "You'll have to hide in the bedroom," she insisted. "And leave after the general and I do." When he looked disinclined to budge, she placed a hand on his arm. "Please, Mitch?"

Although he still wasn't wild about the idea, Mitch rationalized that at least if he was in the other room, he'd be able to protect Tory in case the general did decide to pounce. Giving her a quick, hard kiss, he slipped into the adjoining room just as the general knocked on the door.

"Why, General Ramirez," he heard Tory say with apparent delight, "what a nice surprise! I wasn't certain you were going to make it back in time."

"There was an accident on the roadway," he informed her. "Fortunately my men were able to move the cars out of the way." His dark eyes took an appreciative tour of her gilt clad body, lingering for an uncomfortably long time on her breasts and thighs. "You look extremely beautiful this evening, La Rubia." His low voice vibrated with hunger. "Every man in the country will envy me when I show up at the reception with you on my arm."

From the gleam in his eyes, Tory decided that she had better get the general out of here now, before Mitch found it necessary to defend her honor.

"You flatter me, General," she murmured, picking up her beaded evening bag. "Shall we go?"

A frown plunged between his black brows. "I thought we might have a drink together first."

Tory imagined that she could hear Mitch grinding his teeth. "I really don't want to be late."

"This is Latin America," Ramirez reminded her. "Where it is fashionable to be late."

Tory's smile belied her escalating nervousness. "Ah, but I'm afraid that I'm an incurably prompt American. And I really hate the idea of keeping everyone waiting."

"They haven't been waiting as long as I have," Ramirez pointed out, his voice edged with irritation. "I've missed you."

Tory looked up at him through lowered lashes. "I've missed you, too, *señor general*," she murmured silkily.

"Later, after our social obligations," Ramirez promised firmly, "we shall get to know one another better."

Tory's answering smile was brimming over with feminine promise. "You've no idea how I'm looking forward to that, *señor general*."

When he heard the door close behind them, Mitch gave in to impulse and slammed his bruised knuckles into the silk-draped bedroom wall.

ALL THE MOVERS AND SHAKERS of La Paz were at the ambassador's fete. Included were members of the press and despite Tory's blistering warning looks, Mitch insisted on hovering nearby like some type of overprotective guard dog.

She had just finished a stilted conversation with a Playa de Palma plastic surgeon and his wife, a local socialite who was beginning to gain some measure of international renown as a dress designer, when the ambassador appeared at her elbow. With him was a man Tory found all too familiar.

"Ms. Cavanaugh," the ambassador said, "may I present Colonel Astor. The colonel has just been promoted to commander of our nearby military base," he informed her. "Colonel Astor, this lovely young songbird is Ms. Pandora Cavanaugh. Or, as she is more popularly referred to in Latin America, La Rubia."

Tory struggled to remain calm as she was subjected to the colonel's measuring gaze. "Colonel," she said, extending her hand, "it's a pleasure. And may I offer my congratulations on your promotion."

"Thank you, Ms. Cavanaugh. And the pleasure is all mine." The ambassador drifted into the crowd, leaving Tory to exchange polite party conversation with the colonel.

"How long have you been stationed in La Paz, Colonel?"

"Two years. Before that I was assigned to a military post in Brussels."

That was where he must have met his European smuggling contact. Brussels was infamous as a crossroads. "You must find La Paz quite a change."

Astor shrugged his uniform-clad shoulders. "I spent several years in El Salvador, Honduras and Colombia. La Paz isn't that different."

"I suppose not," Tory murmured thoughtfully, wondering precisely how many tons of artifacts the man had managed to plunder over all those years. "Of all the countries in Latin America, I find La Paz to be the loveliest."

He rubbed his square, Dick Tracy jaw. "I hadn't realized that you'd been here before."

"I haven't."

"Then I assume you've found time to do some sightseeing?"

"Not really," Tory said quickly. "Actually all I've experienced is the city. But it's quite lovely. And so cosmopolitan."

"Yes, it is," Astor agreed absently, as if concentrating on something else. "Then you haven't been to the mountains?"

"No, I'm afraid I haven't had time."

"You should," he said. "The scenery, with its cloud forests and volcanoes, is stunning." Although his lips were smiling, his steely eyes were narrowed intently; he seemed to be struggling with some annoyingly elusive memory. To Tory's relief, the colonel appeared unable to recognize her as the woman he'd met in the mountains.

"I attended your opening night," he informed her, as if putting the puzzle aside. "You were very impressive."

Tory bobbed her blond head. "How very nice of you to say so. I'm flattered."

"It's the truth," he affirmed. "Will you be treating us to a performance tonight?"

"I've promised the ambassador that I'd do a short set," she said. "However, I must apologize ahead of time for my voice. I'm afraid I'm coming down with a cold."

"I know just the cure." He turned to the nearby bartender and ordered a glass of champagne and orange juice. "Vitamin C," he told Tory, handing her the tall mimosa. "Works every time."

Although Tory usually didn't drink before a performance, she didn't want to create a scene by refusing. "Thank you, Colonel," she said. She sipped at the drink, pleased to discover that the orange juice was fresh. The alcohol seemed to numb her nerves, allowing her to continue to exchange cocktail-party conversation with Astor.

She had just finished the drink when the ambassador formally introduced her to the guests gathered in the mansion's ballroom. When the piano player hit an opening arpeggio, Tory set down her empty glass on a nearby table.

As she approached the front of the room, Tory failed to see Astor pick up the glass, wrap it in a linen napkin and slip it into his pocket.

12

TORY'S COLD only made her voice huskier and sexier. After accepting the compliments of the guests, she walked onto the balcony for some fresh air.

Mitch immediately appeared beside her. "Are you all right?"

"I'm fine."

"You looked a little flushed when you were talking to the Peruvian consular officer."

Tory wondered if this man's sharp eyes missed anything. "It must have been the alcohol."

"You drank? With antihistamine in your system?"

"You don't have to bark at me," Tory complained. "I didn't want to, but the colonel insisted. And it was only one mimosa."

"I saw you talking to the guy," Mitch acknowledged. "Did you have to risk blowing your cover that way?"

Tory lifted her chin and met his challenging look straight on. "I didn't have any choice. The ambassador introduced us."

"So how did things go? Did he suspect anything?"

"Of course not," Tory said, not quite truthfully. There had been that one moment, when she'd seen him looking deep into her green eyes and felt that recognition had nearly stirred.

"You're getting out of here," Mitch ordered. "Right now."

Tory was, for once, in no mood to argue. "I'll find Ramirez."

"Fine. And I'll follow you back to the hotel in case you have any trouble getting rid of the guy."

Although Tory would not have wanted to admit it, the idea of Mitch being nearby when she returned to her hotel suite with General Ramirez was undeniably reassuring.

Unfortunately, leaving the reception turned out to be more difficult than she had imagined. Try as she might, she could not locate Ramirez. She was just about to give up the search when she glimpsed him in an adjoining office, talking with Astor. From their agitated expressions she sensed that something had gone wrong.

Mitch had been following Tory's futile hunt for the general when a white-gloved marine appeared at his elbow. "Telephone call for you, Mr. Cantrell," he said.

"I'm a little busy right now. Would you take a number?"

"I'm sorry, sir," the marine replied, "but the caller insisted that it was an emergency."

It had to be Slater. Obviously he'd come up with something important. Deciding that Tory would not leave without making sure he was behind her, Mitch followed the marine down the hallway.

Backing quietly away from the office, Tory went looking for Mitch, who now also seemed to have vanished. She was looking for him in the garden when Ramirez approached.

"I'm afraid that yet another unforseen emergency requires my immediate presence," the general informed her.

"Don't worry about me, General," Tory said. "Someone else can take me to the hotel."

"But my dear," Ramirez pressed smoothly, "a gentleman always sees the lady home."

"Really, *señor general*," Tory demurred, "that isn't necessary. I understand how precious your time is, with tomorrow's election only a few short hours away."

The general's teeth flashed beneath his ebony mustache. "You are a very understanding woman, La Rubia."

Relief flowed over her. "Thank you, General."

"So let us see if you understand this." Grabbing her arm, he pressed a gun against her side. Frantically glancing around for Mitch, Tory realized that she had no choice but to accompany Ramirez to the limousine waiting at the curb. Chivalry was abandoned as he pushed her into the back seat.

"I should have realized you'd be in on this," she complained when she saw Astor waiting in the car. The limo pulled away from the curb, and she searched feverishly for door handles. But they had been removed. She was effectively a hostage.

Tory could only hope that Mitch, ever vigilant, had witnessed her kidnapping and was even now following them.

Mitch was desperately searching the party for Tory, immediately suspicious when his so-called emergency call turned out to be nothing more than dead air. He had just decided to have his friend on the police force check out the hotel, when the marine called him to the phone a second time.

"We have your slut, Cantrell," the masculine voice hissed over the wires. "If you want to see her alive again, you are to tell no one what has happened."

"Is she all right?" Mitch demanded. "Let me talk to her."

The other man ignored his question. "Return home. Do nothing, and wait for our call."

The line went frustratingly dead.

THE LIMOUSINE wound its way through dark and deserted streets outside the city. Tory was terrified. But she reminded herself that she'd been in dangerous situations before and had escaped. The thing to do was remain calm. And not lose her head. Her only hope was to brazen things out and stall until Mitch could find her.

Schooling her voice to a haughty composure she was a very long way from feeling, she said, "Really, General, if you were so desperate for feminine companionship, all you would have needed to do was ask. It certainly wasn't necessary to kidnap me."

"As appealing as you admittedly are, *señorita*," the general retorted, "I am no longer interested in sleeping with you." His dark eyes raked over her, lingering on the long expanse of gilt-clad thigh. Rubbing his chin, he seemed to reconsider. "At least until we discover who you really are. And what you are doing here in La Paz."

"I'm Pandora Cavanaugh," Tory insisted. "La Rubia. An entertainer, nothing more."

"Liar." The general's hand shot out with lightning speed, striking the side of her face with the sharp report of a gunshot.

Tory's cheek felt as if it were on fire, but she would not give Ramirez the satisfaction of letting him know how badly he'd hurt her. Refusing to lift her hand to the throbbing spot, she said, "You are mistaken, *señor*."

"If that's the case," the general responded, "then explain how it is that the fingerprints on your champagne glass match those of a woman the colonel met in the mountains, not far from my Monteverde compound."

"I don't know what you're talking about," Tory insisted.

"You left your fingerprints on the box of Kleenex," Astor broke in. "But you weren't a blonde that afternoon." Reaching out, he whipped off her wig.

To Tory's chagrin, the general recognized her immediately. "Well, well, if it isn't Señorita Tory Martin."

"You have a good memory," Tory muttered.

"It would be difficult to forget you, *señorita*," the general responded. "You were, after all, the only woman reporter covering my revolution.... Where are the papers?"

"I don't know what you're talking about."

He hit her again. Harder. "I think you know exactly what I'm talking about," he countered. "Not that I'm worried," he assured her with an arrogance Tory found hateful. "By now your lover has learned that we are holding you hostage in exchange for the information he has stolen from us."

"And after he returns what we want," Astor broke in as the limousine left the road and turned onto the runway of a deserted airfield, "we will kill him."

"Like you tried to kill my sister?" Tory asked scathingly.

Ramirez gave her a blank look. "What are you talking about?"

"My sister. Amy Martin." Tory was outraged that Amy could have been so foolish as to give her heart to this man, to whom she had obviously meant so little. "The singer at the Hotel de la Revolución. The one you paid to have run down in the street."

"Ah." The general nodded. "I should have made the connection as soon as I realized your identity, Señorita Martin. As for your sister, she was a blackmailer. And a *puta*."

"Amy is not a whore. And she wasn't really blackmailing you," Tory insisted hotly. "She only wanted to be your wife."

"She wanted to be first lady of La Paz," the general corrected. "Your sister was a woman of little principles, *señorita*. She found power and wealth—and those of us who possess it—exciting. Unfortunately she forgot her place."

"So you paid to have her killed."

"That was an accident."

"It was attempted murder, General," Tory returned icily. "And you're going to pay for it, if it's the last thing I do."

He laughed at her impotent fury. "You are a far more intelligent woman than your sister, Señorita Martin." He ran a finger slowly down the side of her face. "And every bit as lovely. But you are also as naively foolish. I own La Paz. What I do in my own country is my business." His expression hardened. "Your sister was fortunate to escape with her life. I fear that you will not be so lucky."

At that moment the car came to a stop and Astor forced Tory out of the car, dragging her across the tarmac to a waiting helicopter. The general stayed behind; it was nearly morning and Tory knew that since the press was scheduled to accompany him to the polls, he could hardly take time from his photo opportunity to commit murder. And why should he? she wondered bleakly. He had so many willing to do the job for him.

The helicopter flew through the night to a compound that judging by the crashing of nearby waves against rocky cliffs was on the Pacific coast. Once they landed, Tory was immediately taken to a storeroom filled with pre-Columbian artifacts. She was bound hand and foot to a narrow cot whose mattress didn't look as if it had been cleaned anytime in the last century. A gag was stuffed into her mouth.

Then the door closed and Tory was alone. In the dark she'd always dreaded.

THE HOUSE had been trashed. Mitch stood in the middle of the living room, staring around at what could charitably only be called chaos. Whoever had ransacked the place had been thorough; they'd slashed open cushions, torn the back off mirrors and pried up floorboards. But they hadn't found what they were looking for. Unfortunately, Mitch reflected grimly, the bastards still had the upper hand. Because they had Tory.

He placed a call to Slater. Then, forced to wait until the abductors contacted him again, Mitch began pacing the floor in an attempt to keep from going crazy.

When the call finally came, three hours later, he scooped up the telephone receiver on the first ring. "Yeah?"

"You are to go to the Medilla plantation outside of town," the voice told him. "Bring with you the papers you have stolen. As soon as we have them, we will release your whore."

The papers were the only thing keeping Tory alive. Mitch was damned if he'd part with them. "Let me talk to her."

"That is impossible."

"How do I know that she's not already dead? Sorry—" Mitch forced his voice into a take-it-or-leave-it tone "—but no deal."

His heart pounding like a jackhammer, Mitch hung up.

TORY TOOK several slow, deep breaths, trying to stop herself hyperventilating. There were mice—or worse, rats—in the room with her. She could hear them scurrying around in the hated darkness. Everything would be all right, she assured herself firmly. She would be all right. All she had to do was figure a way out of this latest predicament she'd gotten herself into.

She struggled with the ropes binding her hands for a long, frustrating time, realizing that escape was a great deal more difficult than all those television magicians made it look on their nighttime specials. Her wrists were rubbed nearly raw when the door suddenly opened and the bare overhead light bulb was turned on. Momentarily blinded by the brightness, Tory blinked, attempting to focus on the shadowy figure filling the doorway.

For a horrifying moment she thought that her moment of execution had arrived, but instead the young soldier merely untied the ropes, jerked her to her feet and pressed a gleaming knife blade against her throat. "You make one move to escape," he said in a low, guttural Spanish, "and I will kill you. Do you understand?"

Still gagged, Tory could only nod.

The guard led her into another room, which she took to be some sort of command center. Three telephones and a computer took up a large part of a wooden desk; nearby was a fax machine, proving that the electronic age was alive and well in this most remote of outbacks. Maps dotted with colored pins covered most of the wall surface, except for an oversize photo of a younger, bearded General Ramirez, appearing appropriately dashing in his rebel uniform.

Colonel Astor unfastened the gag. "Assure your lover that we're treating you hospitably," he instructed, thrusting the telephone receiver into her hand. "And tell him that he must do as we say."

It was bad enough that she had got herself into this fix. Tory was damned if she was going to lure Mitch into a horrible trap. "Mitch," she said, clutching the phone tightly against her ear, as if she could lessen the distance between them. "Don't give in. Whatever they say."

"Wrong answer." The colonel cocked his gun. "Now try again."

"Tory!" Mitch shouted at the sudden silence. "Are you still there?"

The barrel of the revolver pressed against her temple. "Yes," she managed. "I'm here. And I'm fine."

"They haven't hurt you?"

"No." *Not yet*, she added silently. "I did my best not to make waves, Mitch, but I'm afraid that I've gotten myself trapped after all. Please do as they say."

The colonel grabbed the phone. "You've got one hour, Cantrell."

"Wait a minute!" Mitch yelled, playing for time. "It'll take me at least that long to get to the village where the papers are hidden."

"Fine. Simply tell me where you've hidden them and I'll send one of my men."

"No way, Astor. You'll get the papers when I get Tory. Not one minute before."

"All right—" the colonel, furious, gave ground "—you've got two hours, Cantrell. One hundred and twenty minutes and not a second more. If you're not at the plantation with the papers by then, your attractive reporter friend dies."

With that he hung up.

As she was led back to the storeroom, Tory could only wonder whether Mitch had understood her veiled hint. It had only been yesterday when they'd discussed the picnic where they'd almost got trapped by the waves. But in the event he hadn't picked up her admittedly vague clue, she realized that if she was going to get out of here alive, she had better figure out a way to do it herself.

The guard was the key. He was young, arrogant, and obviously proud of his position in the general's elite personal corps. He'd also been raised in a culture that encouraged machismo, an attitude that didn't allow him to consider Tory, a mere woman, a threat. Especially not when she was weeping, as she proceeded to do now.

"Please," she said as they reached the door, "I need to go to the bathroom." Looking at her captor through wet and tangled lashes, Tory did her best to look both embarrassed and chastened.

He gave her a long, considering look.

"Please, *señor*?" she repeated.

Making up his mind, he led her to a door at the end of the hallway. "I will be waiting right outside," he warned.

The moment she was alone, Tory leaned against the door and took several deep, calming breaths. Then she looked around the compact room, frustrated when she discovered the narrow window barred. Vowing that whatever happened, she would not let them lock her into that pitch-black storeroom again, Tory flushed the toilet, ran water into the sink and exited.

Entering the storeroom, they passed shelves filled with plundered artifacts. Deciding that this was her only chance, Tory pretended to stumble. She reached out as if to regain her balance, grabbed a fat stone fertility figure and before her guard realized what had happened, hefted the heavy figure with both hands and brought it down upon his head. Afraid that he might regain consciousness, she managed to drag his limp body to the cot, tied him to the metal legs with the ropes he'd used to bind her, then stuffed the filthy gag into his slack mouth.

Hardly daring to breathe, she slipped out the back door, made her way across the compound, hiding in the shadows, then began running. For her life.

THE ARMY HELICOPTER landed far enough away from the general's Pacific compound to keep the soldiers from hearing the sound of the rotors. "Are you sure this is the place?" the pilot asked.

"It damn well better be," Mitch said. "Because we don't have time to try anywhere else."

"Good luck," the pilot offered.

"Thanks. I'll need it," Mitch muttered. He left the helicopter, ducking his head to avoid being decapitated by the swirling rotor.

As he made his way along the precipitous coastline, so like the one where he and Tory had picnicked eight years ago, Mitch told himself that he had to be right. She'd been trying to remind him about the waves. The high tide. And according to Slater, this was Ramirez's only compound on the Pacific coast. She had to be here. He couldn't allow himself to think otherwise.

Then he saw her. Running toward him.

Tory was just congratulating herself on her successful escape when she saw a man looming out of the fog. Frightened, she began to run in the other direction.

Unreasonably frustrated, Mitch, not wanting to call out to her for fear of attracting attention, broke into a run, easily catching up with Tory.

"Sweetheart," he said, grasping her arm and spinning her around, "you can stop now. It's me."

Looking into his face, Tory felt faint with relief. Unable to speak, she merely clung to him.

She felt so good in his arms. Mitch wished they could stay like this forever. Unfortunately, they were not yet out of the woods. "I think we'd better get out of here," he said against her hair. "Now."

They were on their way back along the cliff, hand in hand, when another man came looming out of the swirling white fog.

"Damn." Mitch recognized the colonel.

Astor was dressed for jogging in a pair of olive drab shorts and a camouflage T-shirt. Although he wasn't wearing a gun, he did have a leather knife sheath strapped to his calf.

"When I give the word," Mitch said to Tory, "I want you to take off running and don't stop until you get to the helicopter. Tell the pilot to take you back to the city as fast as he can."

"That's the same thing you said back at Monteverde. And for your information, nothing's changed. If you think I'm going to leave you out here alone, you're crazy."

Mitch took hold of her shoulders and shook her. Hard. "Dammit, Tory, for once in your life could you just do what I say and not argue?"

Before she could answer, the colonel had unsheathed his knife and approached them with a lazy, arrogant stride.

"I thought that might be you in the helicopter, Cantrell," he said. "But I couldn't figure out how you knew where your little songbird was." His gaze cut to Tory. "I assume you tipped him off somehow." Astor shook his head. "I'm afraid you're going to have to pay for that little trick."

"Now," Mitch told Tory, pushing her behind him with a force that made her stumble to her knees. "Get going."

But Tory had no intention of going anywhere. Not while Mitch was in danger. Regaining her balance she watched, her eyes wide with fright, as Astor lunged, the polished knife blade flashing in the early-morning light.

"Dammit, Tory!" Mitch yelled, managing to dodge the vicious thrust. "Get the hell out of here!"

The two men crouched and circled, and Tory's horror grew. This was all her fault. If she hadn't come to La Paz in the first place, if she hadn't got Mitch involved in her revenge scheme, he wouldn't be fighting for his life.

The blade flashed again, slashing open Mitch's shirt sleeve. When Tory saw dark red blood begin to soak the cloth, she began desperately searching for a weapon. All she could find were the small rocks underfoot, so she scooped them up by the handful and began throwing them at the colonel.

"Dammit!" Astor exclaimed and lunged again. The blade whistled impotently past Mitch's ear. "When I finish your lover off, I'm going to find out if you're as sexy as your alter ego, La Rubia," he promised. This time it was Mitch who lunged, grabbing at Astor's arm. The colonel easily sidestepped him. "And after I'm finished, I'm going to turn you over to those soldiers back at the compound. Then if you're still alive after they have their fun with you, I'll kill you myself."

The idea that this man would even dare to touch Tory made Mitch's blood boil, but he forced himself to remain calm, reminding himself that the colonel was a much more skillful fighter. The man had years of training in hand-to-hand combat; he'd killed people.

Tory refused to let Astor's threats deter her. She continued to hurl her rocks, hitting him around the head and shoulders. One particularly lucky throw struck the hilt of the knife, practically knocking it from the colonel's hand.

"That's it!" he roared. Frustrated, wanting to end this once and for all, he lunged yet again at Mitch, who deftly evaded the attack. The colonel's final startled, furious shout was carried away by the sea wind; he plunged over the rocky precipice into the turbulent surf below.

Tory stared at the spot where the colonel had been standing only moments before; alternating waves of horror and relief washed over her. Dropping her remaining stones she rushed toward Mitch, her fingers gripping his shirt. "You're bleeding!"

"It's only a scratch."

"But it's soaked all the way through. You have to take your shirt off and let me see—"

Dragging her to him, Mitch cut her off with a long kiss. "I'll be fine," he insisted. "Although once we get back to the city, I'd be more than happy to let you nurse me back to health." He pressed another quick hard kiss against her protesting lips. "I have this feeling I'll be needing a lot of bed rest. But for now . . ." He glanced toward the compound, where from the activity of the soldiers it was obvious that Tory's escape had been detected. "I think we'd better get out of here."

The soldiers were running toward them, automatic weapons drawn. Just when Tory thought they'd finally run out of luck, the sky filled with U.S army helicopters.

Faced with the superior firepower of the helicopters' guns, the soldiers put down their weapons. When the first copter landed, James Slater emerged.

"Nice day for a stroll on the beach," he casually greeted Mitch and Tory. "So where's Astor?"

"He decided to take a swim," Mitch answered.

Slater shrugged. "It's probably just as well. The trial wouldn't have been pretty. For either the army or the government." He glanced at Mitch's tattered, blood-stained shirt. "I suppose we'd better get you back to the city, pronto, Cantrell. After all, it wouldn't do for the network's hotshot foreign correspondent to go on the air looking like a bum."

The rising sun was splitting the misty morning clouds with dazzling rays of scarlet and gold. It was going to be a beautiful day for an election. Hot story aside, Mitch was grateful to be alive.

He put his good arm around Tory. "Come on, sweetheart," he said. "Let's go home."

13

As soon as they arrived back in Playa de Palma, Tory called in her story to the Associated Press bureau chief, who, after lecturing her on her dangerous subterfuge, congratulated her on her scoop and assured her that this time she'd win the coveted Pulitzer. Although the idea pleased Tory, she wasn't as excited as she once might have been by such praise. She realized that her time with Mitch was rapidly drawing to a close.

First getting his wound cleaned and wrapped, Mitch spent the rest of the day visiting the various polling places and campaign headquarters, compiling interviews for his own report.

Later that evening Tory turned on the television in her hotel suite and watched Elena Castillo deliver her victory speech. Against all odds, the woman had captured an overwhelming percentage of the votes, proving all the pollsters and political pundits wrong. Tory, always on the side of the underdog, definitely approved.

The new president vowed to bring democracy and political reform to La Paz, then the cameras switched back to Mitch, clad in a clean shirt, his wounded arm in a sling. Tory watched with a mingling of pride and love as he announced the arrest of General José Enrique Ramirez for artifact smuggling. When he went on to explain that Victoria Martin, a crack foreign correspondent for the Associated Press had been the one to uncover the story, Tory beamed.

Cutting to a shot of the general being arrested by an officer of the La Paz national police force, Mitch returned to the screen to inform viewers that after his trial in La Paz, the general would be extradited to the United States for trial on conspiracy charges stemming from the attempted murder of a U.S. citizen. At the welcome news Tory felt the burden of revenge finally fall from her shoulders.

"Are you sure you're all right?" she asked anxiously when Mitch returned to her hotel suite, accompanied by a white-jacketed room-service waiter bearing a bottle of champagne and a silver plate of chocolate-dipped strawberries.

"Never been better."

"But your arm—"

"Will be fine in a couple of weeks," Mitch assured her, going onto the balcony to open the champagne. "Besides, this isn't the first time I've been hurt chasing down a story. And it probably won't be the last."

Tory sampled one of the strawberries, finding it delicious, as expected. Mitch had never been one to scrimp when it came to romantic gestures. "What are you going to do now that the election is over?" she asked.

Mitch poured the champagne into a pair of flutes and handed one to Tory. "I've been thinking of going to Eastern Europe for a while. History's being made over there. I'd like to watch events unfold.... Here's to one of the rare stories with a successful ending."

Ending. As Tory sipped the sparkling wine, she experienced an unhappy feeling of déjà vu. They'd been through this goodbye scene before. Nonetheless, although it hurt even more this time, Tory wouldn't have traded the past week for the world.

"I couldn't have done it without you." She sat down and looked out over the gentle, sunset-reddened Caribbean waters.

"That's not true." Sitting down beside her, Mitch stretched his long legs. "We were both working on the same story from different angles. The way I see it, Victoria, we make one helluva team."

The gleam of appreciation in his blue eyes warmed her to the core. "We do, don't we?" she murmured.

"So what about you?" Mitch asked. "Where do you go from here?"

Tory shrugged. "I haven't given the matter much thought. Perhaps I'll return to Lithuania. Or Estonia. Or wherever the AP decides to send me."

Mitch refilled her champagne glass. "Don't you ever get tired of living such a gypsy existence?"

There was something in his tone. Something Tory could not quite discern. Realizing that this might be the most important conversation she'd ever had in her life, Tory chose not to lie.

"No. You know me, Mitch. I love the travel, the excitement, and most of the time even the danger. And although someday I may want to settle down, there's still too much of the world to see. Too many stories to write."

Mitch sipped his own champagne thoughtfully for a long, silent time. "Still, don't you ever get fed up with being at the beck and call of the AP?"

"I wish I had more autonomy. But there aren't a lot of choices, really, are there?" she asked, wondering what he was getting at. "After all, the network even puts restraints on you."

"And that's been bothering me a lot lately." Mitch popped a strawberry into his mouth. "During those five years I was held hostage, I became acutely aware of the preciousness of each day."

"I can certainly understand that."

"I suppose that's why I find myself chafing under the admittedly benign restraints the network insists on putting on me." He took another drink of champagne.

"You're not thinking of quitting, are you?" Tory asked disbelievingly.

"Of course not. All I want is to live every day of the rest of my life as I want to live it. Free of outside controls."

Tory sighed. "That sounds marvelous. But impossible."

"Not impossible." Mitch put down his glass, rose to his feet, put his hands upon the balcony railing and stared at the sea. "Ever since I was freed, I've had a recurring idea about establishing an independent news production company."

Intrigued, Tory joined him at the railing. "A freelance organization?"

"Exactly. You know as well as I do that budget crunches are causing the networks and wire services to cut back on their foreign offices. The opportunities for free-lancers are limitless. And the time is right."

"It's a brilliant plan."

"I was hoping you'd think so." Mitch flashed her a grin, pulled something out of his pocket and handed her a folded piece of paper.

"What's this?"

"It's a partnership agreement. Since we've already determined that we make a terrific team, I can't think of anyone I'd rather go into business with."

Tory skimmed the brief agreement. "There's no term stated."

"Actually," Mitch said, his calm voice belying his runaway heartbeat, "I thought perhaps we'd begin with fifty years and take it from there."

Tory stared at him, hoping against hope that she had not misunderstood his overly casual words. Before she could ask if Mitch was actually proposing, a trio of mariachis gathered beneath the balcony and began singing a medley of romantic ballads.

"Gracious," she murmured weakly. "You definitely haven't lost your flair."

He put his arm around her waist and drew her to him. "Just wait," he promised.

A split second later, the mariachis' song was suddenly drowned by the deafening noise of firecrackers on the beach—dazzling red, yellow and green flares spelling out I Love You Victoria Martin.

"Oh, Mitch," Tory breathed.

Vastly relieved that he hadn't misread her feelings, that this time she wasn't going to walk away, Mitch took her hand in his. "There's a big, wide, wonderful world of adventures waiting out there, Tory. But I've discovered that they've lost their power to excite me unless I can share them with you."

Tears of joy and love streamed down her face and went unnoticed. "Oh, yes." Laughing, she flung her arms around his neck. "Yes, yes, yes."

Much, much later, lying blissfully in the arms of the man she loved, Tory decided that of all the enterprises she and Mitch had shared and of all those yet to come, love was without a doubt the most thrilling adventure of all.

Harlequin Intrigue

QUID PRO QUO

Racketeer King Crawley is a man who lives by one rule: An Eye For An Eye. Put behind bars for his sins against humanity, Crawley is driven by an insatiable need to get even with the judge who betrayed him. And the only way to have his revenge is for the judge's children to suffer for their father's sins....

Harlequin Intrigue introduces Patricia Rosemoor's QUID PRO QUO series: #161 PUSHED TO THE LIMIT (May 1991), #163 SQUARING ACCOUNTS (June 1991) and #165 NO HOLDS BARRED (July 1991).

Meet:

Sydney Raferty: She is the first to feel the wrath of King Crawley's vengeance. Pushed to the brink of insanity, she must fight her way back to reality—with the help of Benno DeMartino in #161 PUSHED TO THE LIMIT.

Dakota Raferty: The judge's only son, he is a man whose honest nature falls prey to the racketeer's madness. With Honor Bright, he becomes an unsuspecting pawn in a game of deadly revenge in #163 SQUARING ACCOUNTS.

Asia Raferty: The youngest of the siblings, she is stalked by Crawley and must find a way to end the vendetta. Only one man can help—Dominic Crawley. But will the son join forces with his father's enemy in #165 NO HOLDS BARRED?

Don't miss a single title of Patricia Rosemoor's QUID PRO QUO trilogy coming to you from Harlequin Intrigue.

HARLEQUIN Romance

This June, travel to Turkey with Harlequin Romance's

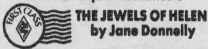

THE JEWELS OF HELEN by Jane Donnelly

She was a spoiled brat who liked her own way.

Eight years ago Max Torba thought Anni was self-centered—and that she didn't care if her demands made life impossible for those who loved her.

Now, meeting again at Max's home in Turkey, it was clear he still held the same opinion, no matter how hard she tried to make a good impression. "You haven't changed much, have you?" he said. "You still don't give a damn for the trouble you cause."

But did Max's opinion really matter? After all, Anni had no intention of adding herself to his admiring band of female followers....

Back by Popular Demand

Janet Dailey
Americana

A romantic tour of America through fifty favorite Harlequin Presents® novels, each set in a different state researched by Janet and her husband, Bill. A journey of a lifetime in one cherished collection.

In June, don't miss the sultry states featured in:

Title # 9 - FLORIDA
          Southern Nights
   #10 - GEORGIA
          Night of the Cotillion

Available wherever
Harlequin books are sold.